Violette Leduc

Violette Leduc was born in Arras, near Lille, in 1907, the illegitimate daughter of a servant and the son of the house. Throughout her life she was tortured by a sense of guilt at her birth, instilled by her mother. It was to her beloved grandmother – the 'angel Fideline' – that she turned for love, but she died when Violette was six. Violette began school at Valenciennes before the First World War, and when her mother married in 1920 such was her distress that she chose to return there as a boarder. Violette's love affair with another pupil, Isabelle, and then with her music teacher, Hermine, eventually led to her expulsion, and she finished her education at Douai and in Paris. Nine years with the devoted Hermine were followed by an unhappy affair and marriage to the masochistic Gabriel, from whom she was separated in 1939. She worked as a press secretary at the publishing house Plon, in a literary agency and for a film company. Living on the peripheries of Parisian artistic life, she met the Wildean figure Maurice Sachs, one of the principle readers for Gallimard. During the Second World War they went to Normandy to live, where Sachs encouraged her to write memoirs of her childhood. During these years she worked on the black market, carrying Normandy produce to the Parisian rich. She published her first novel, *L'Asphyxie*, in 1945, earning her the acclaim of Simon de Beauvoir, Camus, Genet and Sartre. Her other works include *L'Affamé* (1948), *Ravages* (1955), *Therése et Isabelle* (1960), *La Folie en tête* (1970) and *Le Taxi* (1971). *La Bâtarde*, her most famous book, was published in 1964. It became an immediate best-seller in France and established her reputation as a major French writer. She died in France in 1972.

By the same author

La Bâtarde (autobiography)
The Golden Buttons

VIOLETTE LEDUC

THE LADY AND THE
LITTLE FOX FUR

Translated from the French by Derek Coltman
and with a foreword by Deborah Levy

PETER OWEN
London and Chester Springs

PETER OWEN PUBLISHERS
73 Kenway Road, London SW5 0RE

Peter Owen books are distributed in the USA by
Dufour Editions Inc., Chester Springs, PA 19425–0007

Translated from the French *La Femme au petit renard*
First published in Great Britain 1967
© Editions Gallimard 1965
English translation © Derek Coltman 1967
This paperback edition 2007
Foreword © Deborah Levy 2007

ISBN 0 7206 1217 9

A catalogue record for this book is available from
the British Library

Printed and bound in Great Britain by
Bookmarque Ltd, Croydon, Surrey

Foreword

Violette Leduc's novels are works of genius and also a bit peculiar. It is not surprising that Jean Genet was one of Leduc's early admirers, as were Simone de Beauvoir and Albert Camus. According to Edmund White's autobiography *My Lives*, Genet and Leduc even made an amateur film together – a re-enactment of a baptism in which Genet, who was an orphan, played the child and Leduc the mother. Both writers were illegitimate, born at a time – Leduc in 1907 – when such things mattered. The theatre of baptism with its narratives of belonging, of being ordained and claimed, must have been very potent to stage. The mind whirls at the thought of what they might have got up to. What a shame the film has been lost. If, as White points out, both Proust and Genet 'were dismantling all received ideas about the couple, manhood, love and sexual roles', I would include Leduc in the rearranging of the social and sexual scaffolding of her time. I don't think she set out to do this. It was just that her life wasn't quite bourgeois or stable enough to do anything else.

Leduc can make this reader laugh out loud at her grand themes: loneliness, humiliation, hunger, defeat, disappointment – all of which are great comic subjects in the right hands. Samuel Beckett could do this, too. It requires a sensibility that is totally unsentimental, a way of staring at life and making from it a kind of tough poetry created in part by not having led an existence that makes one believe that the so-called compassionate and tender have any pity.

However, it is female love and desire that are Leduc's main subjects. She herself stated that she wanted to express 'as exactly as possible, as minutely as possible, the sensations of physical love'.

In *The Lady and the Little Fox Fur* it is the sensation of hunger, of loss of a future, of everyday connection to the rhythms of busy Parisian life that concerns the old lady of the title. 'She was breathing the oxygen meant for people who had spent their day working. To cry out that it was impossible to begin her life all over again would be useless.'

Leduc's starving old woman isn't really old by today's standards. Nevertheless we are told she 'was handling her sixtieth year as lightly as we touch the lint when dressing a wound'. It is because Leduc profoundly understands how mysterious human beings are that her attention as a writer is always in an interesting place. Her old lady gazes at a calf's tongue in a butcher-shop window and asks herself, 'What was there on a calf's tongue?'

It reminds her of fine sand on the petals of a yellow rose, which makes her think of painting sunsets in her younger days. Her paintings were her equivalent of 'altars and sacred wafers'. Leduc does not sanitize and flatten a perception and make it more literal than it is; she accepts its own language. Life, like language, is coherent and incoherent, and Leduc knows the only way to do justice to this dynamic is to fold into the texture of her narrative the strange in-between bits of experience.

She is incapable of coming up with a boring sentence. There may be a gushing sentence now and again, perhaps, when she forgets to take a breath and hyperventilates on the page. But even that's quite exciting. Evelyn Waugh's definition of fiction as 'experience totally transformed' or Hanif Kureishi's astute observation in *My Ear at His Heart* that writing is often a substitute for experience, a kind of daydreaming, are fair enough but not completely true for her. Writing for Leduc is a concentrated form of experiencing. She is a present-tense sort of writer, and like Virginia Woolf she wants to record 'the atoms as they fall upon the mind'. When her old lady wakes up thirsty one summer morning in Paris she wants to find an orange to suck. So she rummages in the bins and discovers a reeking fox fur in a box labelled tripe. Instead of an orange she had found 'a winter fur in summer'.

She picks it up and takes it home. What does she do with it?

'She kissed him, and then went on kissing him, from the tip of his muzzle to the tip of his brush. But her lips were cold as marble: in her mind these kisses were also an act of religious meditation.'

I laughed at these lines. You are really crazy, Violette, I thought to myself. And then I read the next few lines, where I learn the writer laughs, too. 'She looked him up and down, then burst into her first fit of uncontrollable laughter: the amusement he filled her with was no less sincere than the love she felt for him.'

Precisely. The amusement Leduc fills this reader with is no less sincere than the admiration she feels for her. Literary provocateurs have always written rather peculiar books, and great publishers have always published them. Much to the delight of readers across a number of generations, Leduc wrote her way out of isolation and invisibility and into the canon of twentieth-century literature. As the old lady remarks at the end of this gentle, bittersweet novel, her 'world consisted of nothing but what she had invented'.

Deborah Levy

The Lady and the Little Fox Fur

Twenty-four, twenty-five, twenty-six, twenty-seven, twenty-eight, twenty-nine, thirty, thirty-one, thirty-two, thirty-three, thirty-four, thirty-five, thirty-six . . . then the roar. The table shook, the coffee beans fell into her lap.

The overhead Métro was an invader she had never grown used to, though it shook her like that every five minutes during off-hours, every two minutes during rush hours. She had to see the cataclysm again, wait for it, follow it, learn it by heart, remember it, accustom herself to its every detail. She had to hurry out to reach the station at exactly the same moment as the train itself. As soon as she had left her room habit took over and told her exactly what she must do: first get to the kiosk where the old woman sells the lottery tickets, sniff

5

the scent of bad luck through one of its chinks,
stand beside the news vendor's shelter, and then at
three o'clock reach the steps of the Jaurès Métro
station, after crossing Boulevard de la Villette
between the lines of silver studs. Once she was
standing in front of *Les Palmiers*, the café on the
corner of Quai de la Loire and Avenue Jean-
Jaurès, habit left her to her own devices again.
There were some young girls going into the café,
and she lowered her eyes – the pavement was as
old as she was.

February was a sullen captive in the afternoon
mist, and the grey streets were melting indistinguish-
ably into the grey street corners. She wandered
around the still empty, still silent Paris-Sevran bus.
On tiptoe, avidly, she gazed through the windows
at the backs of the seats, at the luggage rack, and
thought of the passengers who were not there,
whom she had ever known. A hundred yards
farther on, the mail vans were setting out to make
their rounds through the Île-de-France.

The pale tinkle of a bell. Who was watching her?
Was it a warning? Like a sleepwalker guided by
her seeing-eye dog, she disappeared towards the
lock gates on the canal at twenty minutes past three.
The little bells around its neck were the church
bells of a town called Sevran that she would never
see. She forced herself to become calm again,
otherwise she would be too hungry. She retraced
her steps back towards *Les Palmiers*, taking care to

keep her distance from it. It was freezing; inside some young girls were drinking Coca-Cola through straws. She walked across Avenue Jean-Jaurès between the lines of silver studs, back towards the news vendor who sat huddled beside the entrance to the Jaurès Métro station while the coins tinkled down into his saucer. A quarter of four. Every day at that same time a bread roll fell at her feet in the gutter. Every day she prepared to pick it up, every day she began wiping her fingers on her dirty handkerchief. For nothing, for a dream. She looked for it on the shade of a street lamp, but the roll was already dangling at the top of a plane tree with the last dead leaf: mirages of hunger. The policeman was inviting the pedestrians over to the other pavement. She accepted, she plunged forward into Paris, and as she made her way over the crossing, she proclaimed her corner of the city was a forest. The trees, weary from the blue weight of the sky, rested their branches on the buses to Béthisy, to Royallieu, to Vaud'herland, to Verberie. The cars and their fuel gave off a scent of mimosa: the mimosa of a convalescence at Menton forty years before. She stepped with the others up on to the far pavement, and the mimosa was falling like snow on the fenced-off temple: the old Porte de la Villette.

The rules of habit were in charge again. Without the rules she would have weakened and stumbled, because the children were all eating their after-school snacks in the street. She clenched her fists and banged them against her stomach to keep her hands from snatching the croissants out of their mouths. Paris – millions of children all clutching the same horns of plenty. The edge of her round hat brushed against the sign of the *Tout gaze bien* café, at 6, Avenue Jean-Jaurès. Her coat was turning green with age. So much the better : it was a proof that her vert-de-gris candlesticks in the pawn-shop had not abandoned her. When the sun came out, there were two torches to light her way, the sun itself and its reflection in the window of Joris', the shop that accepted la Semeuse coupons. She hummed in the crystal winter and retraced her steps once more. Suddenly she found that she was holding herself back by clutching tightly on to her handbag, the handbag she had always darned with Chinese silk – in the days when she had been able to afford Chinese silk. As she stood trembling, as she squeezed it to her, as she crushed it out of shape, her handbag wanted what she wanted. Her childhood in the country, suddenly brought back to her by the doorway between *Achilles'*, the shut-up café, and Joris', the coupon shop, was making her head swim. Her teeth were chattering and she moaned nostalgically at at the sight of the signs on each side of the porte-cochere, two shields on which she read : *G. Raymond. Legal proceedings initiated. Defences undertaken. All courts. Open daily for consultation.*

8

She kneaded her poor handbag, she moaned entreaties to G. Raymond. How could he not be interested in her provincial past, since he was defending the provinces with his shields. She buttoned up her gloves, forgetting that the press-studs were worn out. On days when her legs would no longer support her, when the pincers of hunger wrenched and pulled out all manner of nails in her stomach, she imagined herself asking G. Raymond to initiate proceedings for her. She imagined them being made to give her bread, and cheese, and wine. The shields shone in splendour. Her handbag resumed its proper shape, she sang the lullaby she'd learned while she was doing her first cross-stitch. Her round hat tilted forward, it fell in front of G. Raymond's door, she stepped on it, she banged her nose against the door because she thought she was going in to see G. Raymond. She stopped her song and let her plan dissolve away until the following day. If her nose bled, she sniffed: she drew sustenance from her own blood. If someone picked up her hat, she said: 'Oh, I am so very sorry.'

There was no pain in her parting from G. Raymond, and she hurried on to the pancake shop. She took up her position outside it to wait for the visitor. Why was it taking so long now, when it came so punctually to crush her in her room, every five minutes during off-hours, every two minutes during rush hours? It must come or she would fall, flattened out on the pavement by the smell of the pancake being turned. I'm waiting for it and it's keeping me waiting, she said to the truck drivers who were staring at her and laughing. There it was. Despite her hunger, despite everything, it made her feel easier inside to see it pierce through the light along boulevard de la Villette, swinging at exactly the right moment round the bend, for her who had no watch. The shuddering of the arches, the vibration of the viaduct was muffled by the noise of the traffic. The roar it made in her room was non-existent as it passed by her up above the square. The thunder was lost: the passers-by had other things on their minds. That cataclysm hurtling past her window towards its terminus, what had it turned into? Into this inoffensive little train from the Jardin d'Acclimatation, with rows of fairy lights along its ceiling. There it went, something that Paris took for granted, something that was simply there. And at that moment she took it for granted too. But before two hours had passed she would be depriving herself of bread for it, she would be buying a Métro ticket so she could be near it and touch it. The stationwoman's signal, that disc waving at the end of a rod, would intoxicate her as keenly as any ocean liner's foghorn.

Wheat pancakes, fifty francs. The batter was spreading across the hot plate, the woman was scraping away the drips and making the edges neater with the point of her knife. But she would draw her nourishment later on from the crowd in

the Métro: one cannot have everything. Of course
the school girls had long hair, coming out of school
was still what it had always been: the beating, the
breathing of the braids against one's back. She
used to plait hers in front of the open window, and
though the lightning flashes used to stab at her
face, still there was something honest about a storm.
But now she had something liked even better than
storms: the delicate drizzle in the park across from
the fenced-off temple, from the old Porte de la Villette. Five schoolgirls bought five pancakes *au Grand
Marnier*. She hadn't changed her mind: the Métro
was better than the pâtisserie. She left, she set off
along avenues, along quais, along streets, along
boulevards, as busy and curious as a dog out on its
own. After turning back and setting off again many
times, she at last reached the place where she wanted
to be: her bollard on the Quai de la Villette. The
swarm inside her left off its buzzing, the warmth
came back into her heart, the sweat on her back
began to dry, her hat fell on to her knees, and her
grey hair came undone. A moment of content-
ment, of self-abandonment as she gazed at what
she had gazed at the day before, and the day
before that: three men near the edge of the water,
beside a sort of greenhouse, hitting their cold chisels
with their hammers. They were workmen whose
job it was to keep the flagstones level, and they put
up with her there because they didn't know she
was there. The bollard she was sitting on had such

stability, the place itself was so historic that she
became a peasant woman who had ridden in from
the Perche country to sell a farmhorse many cen-
turies ago. He will be easy to sell: he has such
strong muscles under that coat the colour of a
baked potato. She sighed a deep, deep sigh and felt
the comfort of it.

Each of the workmen was riveted to his work-
bench – a rusty barrel – hammering out of time
with the others. They were making her a gift of
their task, they were wholly immersed in it. The
Percheron horse and the peasant woman had
crumbled into nothing long, long ago right there
where one day she too would crumble into nothing. Contemplating that thought became a well-
earned rest. Her hands shook these days when she
was threading a needle; her fingers were growing
old; life and death were two maniacs locked in a
well-matched struggle. The iron grille nearby, the
boat stagnating below the quai, the sweepings floating on the ancient water . . . She melted into the
landscape: it became an extension of her own idleness for a while, until the sound of a bus starting
up behind her, the rhythm of its turning motor,
brought her back to life. Her eyes stared straight
ahead for a moment more before coming back to
the hat on her knees, to the loose hair falling about
her shoulders. A flagstone slightly off from the flagstone next to it caught her attention. A slit throat:
the flagstone let a beam of sunlight shine on to her

through its wound. The bollard would be there to-morrow.

At five-twenty she was resting from the streets and their noise in the Citroën waiting-room, going from bench to bench picking up the newspapers that she would then read and reread for weeks on end. She made a tour of the room, inspecting the traces left by passengers now on their way to Meaux, to Souilly, to Claye, to Nangis; orange peel, an empty sweet packet, the cellophane from a packet of cigarettes, a blackened match. They must be kind people, all these fugitives, since they left her these things to remember them by. She would have collected everything they had left and taken it away with her if the ticket clerks had not been watching. But instead she sat down again, hoping that the newspapers she was pressing against her stomach would warm her up. A traveller came in, one vague and solitary man : she heard the clash of cymbals that heralded another presence amid the spectres and the damp stains on the walls. But the solitary traveller was immediately overcome by a dizzying attack of shyness and left again even more quickly than he had arrived. She began putting problems to herself. Not to leave her own neighbourhood, not to travel was a tragedy. But to leave all that she cherished would be another tragedy. Also, what was the point of leaving, since there was no longer for her a distinction between those packets of white mints and a line of chalk cliffs?

Later, down by the canal, she stamped her feet near the lock gates and hugged the big newspapers to her overcoat like layers of aprons. An impressive barge allowed her to yearn for it as she stood, just quietly existing, in the company of a plumber and a workman from the gas company. Her father, swathed in goatskin, drove by in a Panhard. Hello, pretty one, she said to a fragment of poster left on a wall: that loose corner of paper she gazed at so intently, an insignificant martyr being curled and uncurled by the wind, was her acquaintance. The dredger must eat more than she ever did if it could afford to throw up so much sand. The barge *Scabre* arriving: everyone's floating hopes of majesty. Leaning on the wall with the others, she was aware that she would feel less hungry if she walked less. Yesterday they had covered up the barge *Ré-01*: oh, the carefully calibrated way of life she had seen measured out, rung after rung, by the ladders lying along the black tarpaulin! The dear old thing was suddenly so gay – the bargee's non-slip boots trotting up and down, the cable being cast off: Antwerp, Amsterdam – the sparkling rudder and the stiff-starched curtains carried the onlookers far off to some distant land. But today the barge was at rest in its slot in the water: ten thousand gliding years of history brought to a halt.

She felt hungry for a chitterling sausage: that was the extent of her personal epic. Hello, pretty one, she said again to her scrap of poster as it

14

curled and uncurled. Why do I feel so much tenderness, she wondered. For whom? Six o'clock. When she was five years old, at dinnertime Nanny would wipe her chin, then her mouth, then her sticky fingers. They were unloading wood at the C.G.E. warehouse, but it was too late, she would not go. How busy she always was, how much sought after everywhere . . . The streets could not live without her, the shop windows she neglected became just so many ruins. Nanny used to do what Mamma told her to; she used to do what Nanny told her to. The handkerchief was passed from hand to hand, her grief was scented with a sachet of lavender. Her forehead was beginning to sweat, her eyes were swimming, she was hungry and, they were calling to her. From afar in her mind she gazed at the swings across from the Porte de la Villette, standing still, yet ready to hurl themselves into motion in front of the old temple. She enveloped them with her gaze as the hoarfrost envelops a hedge on the first really cold day of the year. Everything outside in the cold was in need of comfort, and her hunger would soon be a tumour inside her. The sight of some men at a bar telling each other what they had been doing that day, their backs to her, gave her the energy to run as far as the cleaner's — for how else could she bear the holes in her stockings, hidden inside the shoes that were much too big for her? The cleaner's on Boulevard de la Villette with its 'Prosperity' machines was not like any of the others. Twenty-five past six, the day was hurtling downhill. A swift good day on the trot to the hampers of shellfish outside *L'huître perlière*. Six-thirty, a snick of shears opening a crate : the pale pinewood of her last resting place was already with her. She bumped into women hurriedly buying food for their dinners; she was breathing the oxygen meant for people who had spent their day working. To cry out that it was impossible for her to begin her life all over again would be useless. The young girl in the cleaner's did not raise her head : she was shutting away the corpses in the machines, transforming the floppy cadavers with her steam iron. Grandpapa, grandmamma, aunts and cousins had given her their blouses, and their shirts . . . The idea that the dead were capable of such generosity put fresh heart into her; it was like a grain of pepper on her tongue. She went over to the open square of window, and there, as the steam from the cleaner's billowed out around her, she lamented softly, very softly for her solitary female state, while her stomach cried out its hunger.

She returned to her post in front of the pancake shop. The placard with the prices printed on it was still the same : Paris had not forgotten her, Paris was lighting up on every side, the night was tender, the light was soft, the neon signs were flickering on, the sky was candid, and she was rewarded for loving Paris so much. Viarmes, Belloy, Saint-

Martin-du-Tertre, Bruyères, Villiers-le-Sec were nothing but the whistling of an errand boy to the
music of the city. She set off towards the Métro
stairs, settling her hat more firmly on her head and
pinning up her silver hair. Unconcerned, detached
from the whole world by her idleness and her age,
she recited the names of all the villages the buses
were going to stop at as she flip-flopped along the
street in her much-too-big shoes, and the recital
became a programme of innumerable happy times
that she had never known.

She sacrificed fifty-five francs for a Métro ticket,
she hummed, she took herself for a little butterfly
before a storm, she walked down on to the platform of the Jaurès station, and trains arrived to
take her on to Strasbourg-Saint-Denis, a station she
usually stayed at a long while. At seven o'clock
she sat down beside the gate to the platform, near
two of the station staff who were chatting together
as they watched the trains coming in and going
out, the passengers arriving and departing, walking
up the stairs and walking down the stairs. She
found reassurance in this ebb and flow. The train
drivers were giving her what she wanted: their
herds of passengers surging past her. But she didn't
want to see their wrinkles, their worries, their sleep-
walkers' gait, their fatigue. No, what she wanted
was their warmth: she had deprived herself of
bread, now they were to give her their warmth in
its place. Motionless, she travelled with them in a

17

tunnel where the typists' fingers, the packers' wrists, the bank clerks' foreheads, the waists of the saleswomen from the shoe shops, the ears of the switchboard operators, and the postmen's feet filled her with wonder. She turned her head to watch a young lady, or perhaps a young man, who sold paisley or cashmere by the yard: she was walking through an Oriental bazaar.

She took her key out of her pocket, she dangled it between her thumb and forefinger, showing it off to them all. They were all on their way home, that was next in their future. She had to move along the seat, they key slipped and vanished; suddenly she was unbelievably alone as she searched for it in her lap. Lowering her eyes, dying, then dying again. Quick, quick she was back in position once more. Her hands fastened again around her handbag, around the tiny sum of money inside it, and for one moment she became their beloved. A spectacle case fell to the ground. A tiny sound in the crowd, and the crowd engulfed her again like a lover. The spectacle case was retrieved: apologies, thanks, politeness, conventional phrases. How urbane everyone was . . . The doors slid together, neatly sealing all the people in. She purred on her bench, she was a cat being stroked by polite phrases exchanged between strangers: 'You're too kind,' 'Thank you so much,' 'You really shouldn't have.' Some teenage boys with enormous eyes were staring at her. Then they were dredging inside her: ahh! A drill, ahh!

a screwdriver, ahh! sharp points, hammers, pincers, hinges, sourness, swelling, shrinking – she was a howling shadow conscious only of her hunger. The mouse between the rails became a quail trotting about on a hearth and turning a beautiful golden brown. She began to see visions. There was no need to be disheartened. She saw men in rags greeting one another at midnight, counting out the coins they had harvested on the café terraces, all behind a curtain of black rain. It wasn't much, and yet it was something vast as well, that money in the hollow of each palm. The few passers-by were hurrying to their warm homes. And she saw herself too, living still in an apartment opposite the Luxembourg. Centrally heated of course. It was comfy, as they say. Memories are comfy too, they are swaddling bands, they wrap you up warm like a mummy. What moment is there in life that is not already a memory?

She came back to the platform on the Strasbourg-Saint-Denis station, she found herself still sitting on her seat and realized that it was time for the multiplication table if she wanted to see him again. Two and two are four, two and two are four, two and two are four . . . No. One and one are two, one and one are two, one and one are two, one and one are two – until the presentiment that he was about to come flooded through her. After the mental arithmetic, her lips began to move : make him come, make him come now. He would come;

there was no torture in asking for his presence in the thunder of a departing train. If the wished-for appearance had coincided with the wish itself, the violence of her pleasure would have set her gazing enquiringly at the backs of men's heads – preferably thickset ones – to see if what she felt was the same as making love. They had been breathing the same air without her knowing it, for suddenly he was there, passing indifferently in front of the seat where she sat, below the squares with all the titles of the plays and shows in them.

The lollipop eater was sitting down, as she had done, taking his place on the same bench, to her left – at the far end, away from her, away from the entrance gate. At first he simply sat there with folded arms, just existing. Just existing seemed to be a duty to him. He wasn't seeing anything. Two exasperated passengers might come to blows directly in front of him, or a woman might scream, and he would never react. Perhaps he was a sandwich man who had finished his day's work. His iron-grey overcoat was well on the way to becoming like the topcoats of those ragged auditors she had seen counting their coins on the dark boulevard between Le Dôme and La Coupole. After this period of gentle existence, he was suddenly hidden from her by a gust of hair, his cheek bitten off by the corner of a flapping poster. She tried to lose herself with him on the poster, caressing a lock of her silver hair with a decorative gesture of flirtation, imagin-

ing herself to be accosting him on a beach where a
southern breeze was always blowing.

It was at that moment every evening that he
stood up and advanced with slow steps towards the
slot machine. He looked at no one. She pictured an
imaginary link between the leaky shoes that were
much too big for her feet and the worn-out boots
he was dragging across the platform with such a
weight of fatigue. She invented dramas, tragic
shadows, because the man's expressionless face was
always concealed behind the mask of those who
cannot use a razor every day. He was not a brother
in poverty but a secretly cherished black sheep. He
was her prophet with nothing to prophesy, but it
was enough that he was there. Some of the passengers turned to look at him before disappearing
through the doors. Should she follow him? Should
she put twenty francs into the machine as he was
doing? Should she buy what he was buying? She
hesitated, feeling a cold sweat break out on her
skin. The story would be over if she went up to
him. No, she would rather watch the five transparent pictures of the five flavoured icebergs, the
fingers unwinding the wrapped, the unreal blue of
the ice stick in the other's hand. He had come
back, or he would come back; she could be sure
of that as soon as she heard the click inside the slot
machine. They sat together on the same bench as
train succeeded train, as she nibbled, as she sucked
through the teeth and drank down the saliva of a

friend to whom she would never speak. One day, she could have sworn it, the lighting on the platform had changed; he looked at her, and then, entirely absorbed by his delicious iceberg, he let his eyes drift away from her again with so much indifference that she felt her own life inside her swinging round the widest, the sweetest of curves. Because he was unaware of the kindness he felt towards her he did not need to look at her: he could see her everywhere! He was meditatively consuming a mint-flavoured lollipop; she was a little mountain pink unfolding her petals. On the days when he produced a second ice stick, when he unwound the second wrapper as diligently as if he were peeling a shrimp, she would lose her head altogether; she would escape into one of the tunnels of the Strasbourg-Saint-Denis station, open out her arms and beat her wings: she was a bird-woman using up her last breath for him. She watched, she waited, she came back on to the platform when he had gone. What was to become of her when she no longer had fifty-five francs to see him again? She shivered in advance.

She did not sit down on the seat again after he had gone. She went over to the train, she stroked the door handles that had been grasped and lightly brushed by thousands upon thousands of passengers. The stationwoman with the 'signal' under her arm waved at her to get into the compartment or else stand back. She did not move. It was the crowd that took the decision for her: the hurricane whirled her back across the platform while she laughed aloud at so much generosity and gazed up enquiringly into the faces of the people who were annoyed. They trampled on her handbag and wrenched a button off her coat. A spitting sound, a whistling sound; the cars shuddered into motion. She gathered up her wreckage.

She returned to her place on the seat. The stationwoman with the signal was tired and sat down beside her to rest between trains. What would she not have given for a feeling of closeness, for a current of sympthy . . . She said good-bye to the punched ticket she had been keeping warm, she slipped it with all the furtive caution of a thief under the stationwoman's thigh: she thought that this Cybele crowned with her stationwoman's cap would smile at her before hurling forward to brandish her signal. The young woman yawned, then leaped up with her disc on its handle; the ticket fell to the ground and twenty pairs of hobnailed boots walked over it, dirtying it – as they would go on dirtying it until one o'clock in the morning. Every time a foot was raised and she caught a glimpse of it, she saw her life callously leaving her, she felt it was doing what children do: sucking her blood. Never mind, she would draw zigzags down the margins of her newspapers, she would listen to the pizzicati in the frizzly hair of the man who sucked his flavoured lollipops in a dream.

She went back to her room; she saw a bug cowering underneath a viaduct, and it was herself. What was to become of her now that she no longer had fifty-five francs left over to go down into the Métro?

Twenty-four, twenty-five, twenty-six, twenty-seven, twenty-eight, twenty-nine, thirty, thirty-one, thirty-two, thirty-three, thirty-four, thirty-five, thirty-six . . . the roar. Her hand shook, the coffee beans scattered across the table. She stood up, the beans in her lap scattered across the floor. She was stricken with panic by all that wasted arithmetic. She tilted the table : the dishes smashed among the coffee beans. As she collected up the broken shards of crockery, she longed to try and nibble at the smallest one; it looked so much like one of the pieces of coconut they sold at the stall just along from Joris', the ten-franc slices they put on a plate. She lay flat on the floor and dislodged the beans under the sideboard with a fork. She imitated the Negro woman and her enormous laugh when she was choosing the coconut with most hair on it. She carried each bean back to the table: thirty-six trips across the room, thirty-six puffs to blow the dust off thirty-six coffee beans. She lined them up on a piece of white paper, glimpsing the meagreness of her resources in each tiny groove. The roar. She was sickened by her own pettiness. She swept the beans off the table with the back of one hand, stepped up on the packing case under the high attic window, and sprinkled all the beans still left in the packet over the floor. The brown hail gave her a sense of importance. It was a promise of opulence. And at the same time she asked herself: why am I doing this? Using her handkerchief as a broom and the lid of a sugar carton as a dust-pan, she began to salvage the beans once more. A lock of hair falling in front of her eyes was an unexpected visit; it reminded her that the electric light in her room would never go out. Now she was cleaning off each bean with the cuff of her nightdress. Like all her personal linen, it was no more than a flock of downy tatters of weightless swans.

She was handling her sixtieth year as lightly as we touch the lint when dressing a wound. She stepped up on the packing case underneath the little window and shook the packet of coffee three hundred times, four hundred times, until she felt that the back of her head was pressed against the stars. It was freezing and the moon was shining.

She was dreaming of the pale milky green of that
February wheat. She was free, she did what she
liked, she told herself that she was just like a whirl-
wind. Sixteen years old: to bathe in a field of
poppies, to feel one's calf and the back of one's
thigh brushed by one of those old, wrinkly petals
with their powers of consolation.

The concierge used to explain it to her: you
can't have Paris without the roar of the Métro
as well, because they go together. The concierge
would think it over quietly, then she would ex-
plode: the tenants got used to it, they all told her
the same thing as they stood there opening their
mail, they all said they didn't know what to do
with themselves now when there was no noise. No,
the concierge said, Paris isn't a forest. If Paris
were a forest it would be boring for everyone. I beg
your pardon, Paris in our neighbourhood is a forest
of buses with the trees of Viarmes and Belloy resting
on their roofs. The concierge didn't listen; she
put up a card on her door to say she wasn't at
home to anyone. The concierge could not waste
her time with silly talk. So why could she not get
used to the noise? She preferred the purring aeroplane up above the cracked walls. Was it not just
a little, perhaps, that she was refusing to get used
to it deliberately? She could remember too well
what tranquillity had been like. Oh it had been a
love, tranquillity. But the overhead Métro – a
grinding of bayonets. Paris can be quiet if one

wants to take the trouble, Paris is not lacking in restful little corners. Paris is a muff when it snows. The concierge would shrug her shoulders because her beef stew had to be seen to, because she had guests coming. Oh, you people with so much time on your hands, you people who can go out every afternoon, the concierge answered another day. She did not dare confess to this guardian so anxious to protect her tenants from complications, from eccentricity, that she also was a guardian, the guardian of a sleepy street, of a street that had grass sprouting between its cobbles, that was always there inside her, her native, childhood wilderness. It was a street chaste as an untold secret: noises grew wan as soon as they entered it; laughter, if it ever found its way in, was impaled on discarded graveyard crowns. She stumbled, she stammered, she tripped over her own apologies: the concierge was wasting her time with her. It was better not to speak at all if she wanted the street to sleep on inside her. The concierge went back into her lodge, still saying that she had no time to lose. But she, she was losing her time as other people lose their jobs or lovers. She walked up the seven flights with lowered head. The Métro that sapped her very being, the Métro to whom she was always faithful was awaiting her. She closed her door. She was cheating the concierge because she could not do without it, because she was expecting revelations from it. Go on, be prophetic for me a little, she

28

murmured in its ear as she listened to the thunder. She brushed her skirt, then stopped when her hand began to shake. She always saw to her clothes after she had been out. Did the concierge whisper nasty things about her to the deliverymen? The overhead Métro didn't whisper: it crushed you, it rushed through you, it ground you to powder every five minutes during off-hours, every two minutes during rush hours.

Five, six, seven, eight, nine, ten, eleven, twelve, thirteen, fourteen, fifteen, sixteen, seventeen . . . How many in a half a pound of coffee? The beans she took out in handfuls from the packet fell into the salad bowl one by one. She counted them, and her concern for economy was so intense that her hand shook with it. She trembled, and her legs gave beneath her. She did too much for one so undernourished. To die after so long a diet. She fed on her own saliva, she tamed her hunger, her head was dripping over one shoulder, her feet were blobs of spittle. The beating in her temples was forcing her eyes shut, the thudding in her ears was wearing her down, she was about to yield. No. The darkness inside her was resting her, it was an unasked-for reprieve.

She opened her eyes again to find that the things in her room had never doubted her. For example: the folding chair she had sat in when she was twelve was still there, just as it had been then, when she sat on the lawn, safe in the folds of her

taffeta dress, listening to her mother vocalizing inside the house. When she sat on the folding chair
now with her severe features, her silver hair, her
modest eyes, she looked like a lady professor on
vacation sitting by the edge of a path. It is not
only streams and rivers that flow : a street, with
a door set back from it, can slide over into the
depths of an abyss. The street was her youth, was
all the minutes, the seconds of her existence. The
grass sprouting between the cobbles, the pinpricks,
the needles while her stomach cried its hunger.
The closed door, the step she sat on – quietly, for
there was nothing she desired. A door set back
from the street was enough for her. To grow old
is to wrap ourselves up well so we can wander
warmly through our private catacombs.

She put the salad bowl on her knees, she was
listening, in the groove of each brown coffee bean,
to the sharp reverberation of the bell beyond the
lawn, beyond the kitchen garden, beyond the
woods and the ploughed fields when she deigned
to come in from her native wilderness. The in-
exorable click of her parasol. Day in, day out, she
was always tearing herself away from what she had
been at eighteen. The roar : her youth was whisked
out of sight in an express. Her calculations, her
meticulous juggling with minute sums informed her
that she was using too much electricity, for one
little spoonful of coffee would be enough for breakfast. There were so many spoonfuls to be counted

in half a pound of coffee, but it was a way of making a future for herself. She snatched up the cane left behind by the previous lodger and searched for more beans underneath the sideboard, a gift from the concierge when she cleaned out the cellar. The scrap merchant didn't come around very often these days, and what's more he had to be begged to take things away. The plates in the cupboard at the bottom shook during rush hour.

The unhealthy heat, our timidity . . . No, that wasn't right. Her timidity : a comfortable lining inside her, a furry slipper that warned her : close up, keep silent, protect yourself, don't give anything away now that they're letting you sit at the table. She used to dirty her napkin at the end of the meal; she just couldn't stop herself. No regrets. She had lost nothing and gained nothing. The collector would threaten her when he came around with the electricity bill. She switched off the light, then walked to and fro in the darkness, crushing the coffee beans underfoot. She would pick them up again later, when she had nothing else left. She switched on the light again; that way it was easier to see the hundred and fifty francs lurking between the two worn-out dishcloths. Even if she had only a centime, she would still hide it. Nothing else left : her future, like an epidemic, getting closer. All those galas among the stars while one counts up to sixty. The sky was inviting her to join its festivities again, and this time she switched off the light with more deliberation.

Mariette, Lisette, Odile. The young ladies whose keyholes belonged to her when they were at work four storeys down. She went out on to the landing and listened to the water dripping there. The three young maids took no advantage of it, for how could such harum-scarums appreciate the maxims of monotony taught by a tap. She smiled at the teacher who was dripping his knowledge for her into a sink. Don't forget your 'Lemon' hand lotion after you've finished with the dishes, young ladies. The young ladies' timetable was a source of satisfaction to her. When they went dancing at night she was there in a cloud of face powder. Several times during the day she waited for them hopefully, standing near the drips of water from the tap. When the young ladies came up the stairs, she fled. On Sunday evenings, Mariette, Odile, Lisette would visit one another before going out again. Where would she be next Sunday, when the hundred and fifty francs were already in other hands? She pressed two fingers against her head, first in one place, then in another. Against her forehead: a stethoscope sounding out her situation. Rusks or ordinary bread? The rusks would cost more but then they would keep. Could she live on a quarter of a rusk a day? People can fast completely for forty-five days without dying, and she always had something to eat every day, no matter how little,

32

so what had she to complain of? And anyway, she could always count on that drop of water continuing to fall at regular intervals. Time was a necklace; each bead a gleam on her grave. The sound of Viennese music drove her from the landing and followed her back into her room.

Still she did not go to bed. She stayed up, sometimes standing, sometimes sitting, sometimes sailing to and fro beneath the attic window draped in the long dressing-gown the concierge had given her. What trouble the concierge had gone to, to give her a present. What thick layers of newspaper it had taken to roll it up in, that dressing-gown once worn no doubt by a foreigner, by one of those eccentrics who play at being nabobs in their leisure hours at home. The lapels had a scent of Chypre and English tobacco, and on nights when there was a moon the brocade would sparkle in its beams. If the moon was hidden by a russet veil, then the martial gestures of her arms declaimed that she was married to a breastplate and a suit of armour. It was her virginity. She lowered her arms; then, quite suddenly, she felt the weight of her head pressing on one hand. What was she? Two closed eyes: the sum of all that had been. The company of her bare feet lit by a moonbeam on the dirty floorboards . . . She sat down on the packing case: her trust in them was so great she could have wept, though they were no more than a pool of paleness on the floor. She listened to the humming sounds she could hear when the silences between them stopped: the marches and the halts along her life's path. A child was still crying in another building; somewhere there was a taxi crossing Paris, the man at the wheel dreaming of a plan for an entire city. The paleness and bareness of her feet: poverty is pity too – it had been snowing on the only primrose while Nanny was taking off her shoes. She stood up on the packing case again, travelling out in search of youth and fragility above the antennae and the chimney pots. That powdering of pink across the sky didn't mean it was dawn; it came from the neon signs. She stood rubbing her stomach, keeping it amused, as all the fruits and the orchards of the sky fell in upon the hotplate of the pancake shop. What she needed was money, that's what she told the cars down below and the deep blue up above as it was crowded farther and farther into its corner by the festivities in the sky. Then, the splendour of a surprise: her wish was caught and carried away by an overhead Métro train.

She took out her hairpins and combed her hair with her fingers, smiling a worn smile at the plank left out on a roof. Sometimes she allowed her thoughts to wander, without troubling to speak. To marry. For an hour or two. The husband would have an inspiration, then the iron stay propping the window open wouldn't be in her way any more. The idea of asking a carpenter to come in and see to it would never enter her mind. She rested awhile on the thought of the potato she would eat to-morrow. She swayed on the packing case, but she refused to notice it: the day she could no longer step up on the packing case to look through the window would mean saying good-bye to her friends . . . The lighted windows beside the darkened windows invited her, welcomed her. She went in through the windows, she penetrated into the phosphorescent antichambers of the people who were expecting her, whom she would never meet. More than friends. The drip-feed of another presence into her blood when an apartment opposite lit up. To miss the appointments they had made for her . . . She would die if that happened; a death we cannot know. Habit is even stronger than love. She was filled with a fixed determination to pay the next month's rent, to sally forth once more to the pawnbroker's, to offer him the clothes off her back, to sell her teeth, her leg, her arm, but at all costs to go on living against the panes of strangers' windows. Other people were her hour glasses: the two old men with red-rimmed eyes who sat at their fifth-floor window for example, and their perpetually alternating plants: the ivy and maiden-hair being taken in, the onions being put out. And on one of the balconies there was a geranium as bright as a cock or a corrida. Then there was the woman on the balcony, especially on Sundays, who leaned out and shouted *au revoir* to her lover. How did she know there was a lover down below? The woman was an aviary; her caresses, her groans set loose whole flights of cooing pigeons. *Padam, padam, padam,* she had once heard a woman in love sing out of a jukebox, and every Sunday now that same tune rippled around this woman's flanks. Other people were her opium. How could she go on finding supplies of the drug she needed once she had been thrown out into the street?

One night, as a train was fleeing from winter outside her attic, a window had been opened by five or six bars of trumpet playing. Then the window had closed again. The diamond winter and the glittering brass. She remembered it still in summer, in the gardens of a square, and she thought of herself as the chosen one of winter. She waited for the brazen blare of jazz again, the first night of frost, but the window would not light up. She bared one shoulder, then a breast before dawn came, turning towards the musician who no longer played for her. What did she have to feed him on? Forty years of solitude and life in the wild. Now it was February, she was expecting him still as the attic window fell shut, as she began to feel cold, as she set fire to the newspapers, as the flames tossed the trumpet and the five or six bars it had played for her from one to another, as she celebrated the talent of the trumpet player by warming herself at the blaze.

She switched on the electric light and watched

the wheel inside the electric meter. The wheel was turning quicker than the earth, while the earth delegated its power of turning to a tooth-edged thing caught in a mousehole. What is there to trust in if time is a little dog chasing its tail, if the needles of clock faces are dead insects . . . The wheel, in conclusion, was torturing time.

She divided up six potatoes between eight days. She could eat three quarters of a starchy tuber every day. The quarter of yellow flesh thus saved would go black, and she would throw it away. She clutched her forehead, her heart was beating even in the backs of her thighs; as she soaked the pencil with her sweat she confessed to it in whispers that she hadn't enough left to buy four pounds of sugar. Eleven o'clock. The roar.

Eleven o'clock. She took off her dressing-gown. She walked around in her long nightdress holding a book; the hours chimed out over a pastoral scene, the landscape was a spectre watching her advance; she was walking over tapestries of tiny flowers; her feet were sending up messages of ecstasy; spring was flying away in clouds of white petals. Day was dawning; how did one set about not being old at seventeen? Now, at sixty, she tells herself that that wasn't living, that it was better than living. A day will dawn. She used to gnaw at her fingernails as the birds covered the monumental mason's crosses with their droppings. A day would dawn. The earth would be all ashes and gaping burns, and she would smile the smile of an accomplice who had known all along. The smoke would rise and, noiselessly, she laughed, her mouth splitting open as far as her ears: she would go on dying forever along with the others. The roar, after eleven-thirty came less often.

She folded the dressing-gown in three, arranging the pillow thus formed on the mattress lying on the floor. She was trembling as she stood there, shivering in the piece of butter muslin that served her as a nightdress. She was not ridiculous: she did not know that such a thing as being ridiculous existed. A sick feeling from head to toe; quickly, half a lump of sugar moistened with a drop of water from the tap. Mariette, Odile, Lisette . . . Gone out without changing. She retreated, then stuck her nose slowly out again, reconnoitring a floorboard, a darkened doorway. She closed her hands over the potatoes that were to last a week. To be like a tuber, to be robed in earth, not to have to support the slow dilapidation of one's entrails. Her hand fell away, the weight of her head was too much for her, a potato rolled under the table. She cried, 'Oh, oh,' for if she did not eat she would float away, and the feeling of being as light as a cigarette paper filled her with panic.

She covered herself with the shawl full of holes, hoping that she would weigh a little more that way. But she was weighing less and less. Lucienne had dreamed that she was floating away, just before she died. She lay down, her feet icy. She would have warmed them up with a hot-water bottle, if only the level of the methylated spirits burner would stay the same. She blew on her hands, or she took some warmth from her armpits and carried it down to her heels.

Several times during the night she would grow uneasy about her bedside table: a shoe box. That was where she had hidden the piece of wood she had found when she was seventeen, just as day was breaking. To give birth to oneself. The day was breaking, she could not escape it. The light comes slowly when it is winter and we are pondering. My boat, she said, as others might say my rosary, my prayers. That shapeless object she had carried about with her everywhere for forty years was the ball, the chains that kept her in bondage to the trees. She has said good night fifteen hundred times to the same mist of branches and twigs. The boat slid from her hands, from the hands of an old woman crumbling away, a crossroads, a meeting place for all the hissing and thumping in the world. My temples, my stomach, she groaned, addressing the words to her feet, to two warm strangers. Her eyes were misting over, her heart was talking on her lips. To need everything when everything is finished. She no longer knew whether she was sad or whether it was hunger. To live like that, head bent forward, chin resting down near her breasts, without muscles, without sinews, without vertebrae.

She smiled a martyr's smile for her own benefit: for her wretchedness was also a tenderness, and resignation is not the same as oblivion. There it was, as punctual as the half hour chiming from a clock, the cube of sugar moistened with rum swaying at the end of its piece of string . . . Tap-tap on her cheeks, there it was; tap-tap on her forehead, there it was again. Even if it were only a half cube of sugar . . . There were moments when she had no saliva left to remember with, not even the pale pink water ices that her parents used to eat. Just a quarter of a cube of sugar . . . Why wasn't she a little doggie? Here is my paw, here is my tongue, here are my eyes, here is the wordless language that they speak, here is my maddening silence. No, there were no takers, and binding her stocking tight round her head did nothing to cure the throbbing. She scattered her limbs across the disorder of the mattress. The roof flew off, and she talked to the owls who do not sleep at night, who gaze down at those who devour and those who are devoured, yet do not see them, and she said: my poor prisoner, if I could set you free . . . you've been in prison for so long . . . Her blood: that was her prisoner. She gathered herself together again and listened with compassion to her pulse. Then she hunched up tight and added that it was a beggar to whom she never opened the door. Why not? Why not open, why shouldn't she sprout feathery, spurting fountains? She sat up and looked. That woman coming towards her, scattering feathers, and jewels, and diamanté, with dripping aigrettes emerging from her navel, from her anus . . . It was herself, it was her blood set free from every orifice. She was still importuned by palpitations of the heart. She was forced to bear with all the young and girlish emotions she had not felt when she was sixteen.

In the silences, longer and longer now, between the roars, she kept intent watch on her room, on the room that every night kept watch on her. Hundreds of little squirrels' eyes, sparrows' eyes, frogs' eyes, toads' eyes, chickens' eyes, chicks' eyes, hens' eyes looked down from the ceiling, trying to make out what she would do, how she would stand up to it. The eyes bred and multiplied till the walls were papered with them : stupidity on the alert, ruthlessness keeping vigil. She fell forward with her head in her arms : thousands of beady chickens' eyes were putting the same question to the back of her neck. Dying wouldn't be so difficult an undertaking; but she would rather just go on being interrogated all the same. They were worse than some farmyard tragedy, those chickens' eyes drilling so spitefully between her own. She drank a glass of water. Suddenly her attention was caught and held by a slight cracking noise, a signal made by a little insect beginning some methodical task in the woodwork of the sideboard or the skirting board. At the same moment, she caught the sound of an aeroplane, flying with its airmail through the sky. It was still possible to purr up in the sky, to fly away, to come back: all was not lost. She caught herself economizing her breath, concentrating on keeping desolation at bay inside her. Despair also meant dilapidation. She swept her forehead, her temples, her eyelids with wide brush-strokes, until she emerged from her mattress, from her room; until all the lights of Paris were giving their performance to one pale flower. The city, despite all its flickering lights, was yielding itself up to the silence of the trees along the avenues, to the desert of the transparent cafés. In a flood of gentleness, the grey statues on the Right Bank and the grey statues on the Left Bank were all posing for the same photographer: the night. The statues were dreaming that they were smiling as the river towed past its vessels built from darkness. She was touching up her picture of Paris. A merry-go-round under a tarpaulin: the epitome of a vast city. The grey monk, the old river, was floating past the gate of a weeping graveyard; the acacia was quivering beside the anthracite saucer of a coalyard; the street in the starveling glow from the street lamps was more than a street: a romance in another world bounded by the two graveyard walls.

Her heart was beating less quickly now, her stomach was listening to reason at last, the level of the methylated spirits in the bottle was still the same, the six potatoes were holding a conference on the table, there were a hundred and fifty francs hiding between the two tea towels, and there were spring mattresses to be bought in bedding shops. Stop there. Spring mattresses only lead one to thoughts of soft eiderdowns and bedcovers. And the hearts of the pastry palm leaves in the restaurants, they may look like iced ivory outside, but inside they too are soft, after you've found a thousand-franc note folded in eight on a pavement . . . She hid under the bedclothes. The total of the bill : nine hundred and sixty francs. She rose back to the surface, dazzled by a meadow filled with gold, a field of cows tearing up buttercups with rasping tongues. She recited her eight-times table with a special emphasis on 8 times 8 is 64; she was blinded by the gilding of a cock on a steeple; she recited *Midi, roi des étés*; she expanded near a red roof, against the blue sky. That young girl closing her parasol, carrying her straw hat slung on her arm by its ribbons, weighing that fleshy bunch of wistaria in both hands without picking it . . . Would no tomb be deep enough to swallow that young girl? She sighed with such conviction that her pillow was suddenly filled with all the sleep of all the sleepers in a dead city. Where was she as she remembered that simply allowing herself to float was more restful, more pleasurable than sleeping? To seek without finding is one way of attaining pleasure. She listened. Tears rolled down her cheeks because the little animal in the wood of the sideboard or in the skirting board would no longer be at his methodical task tomorrow. If the room had been less resigned she would have sobbed. Where would she be in a week's time? She went straight off to sleep, then woke up again five minutes later. The insect had stopped its noise. Her room . . . it was filled with does, opening and closing their flirtatious eyes. No, it was only the night. Paris, ah, Paris in a silent film, Paris wrapped in Judex's cloak. The building across the way didn't play these tricks on her; it was grappling with the silence. She drank another glass of water, then buried her pretty little nose in the empty glass. That was her way of shutting herself off, of shutting out her memories.

She might have saved herself the trouble: the memories were in her glottis too. The man who sold futures would be back in early autumn with the metal hand. He took yours and placed it palm down against his metal one. He came in a caravan, bringing his envelopes, ringing his bell. The bell was more leaden than the one outside the Eden cinema, but it could sound very like it if the wind was coming from the right direction, if the gutters had frozen over before it was time for the performance to begin. His bell told all the people that he'd arrived; a shivering foretaste of the futures he had brought them. She used to watch it all, but the only thing she liked was the metal hand because its out-spread fingers had such purity of line. She pre-ferred the tenant in the building, the man who trafficked in light and darkness before the first Métro train. He got up before the others, this pioneer, he recreated noise for her, and gestures, and movements, and socks and clothes and hygiene before finally banging the heavy outside door of the house behind him : a whole day over before the dawn had even broken. She must avoid turning over on her mattress. Five to one in the morning is not a kind time; it is a harsh master. The shawl slipped off, the water in the glass spilled, the dressing-gown folded in three became recalcitrant. She made herself soft, she tried to be as inert as a lump of lead.

Mariette, Lisette, Odile would be coming in and going to their separate rooms. They weren't going to be a bundle of blackened seaweed that the sea has left behind in a room, on a mattress on the floor – but yes, there was something she loved. She loved Mariette's and Lisette's and Odile's sleep. One o'clock. The ticket collectors were closing the zip-fasteners of their hold-alls. Caterpillars were safe inside their chrysalises. Something else she loved : this respite from the noise. Paris in repose, Paris a victory for those lying wounded. The day after tomorrow she would imitate the rabbits, she decided; she would live on the outside leaves of cabbages. She's an eccentric, her father and mother

45

had always said, but there is no such thing as eccentricity: there is what is. She would like to scorn the whole world since the whole world scorned her. Could the old stocking still bound round her forehead tell her what she is? Yes, dried cow dung clinging to dried thistles. She applauded and shouted 'Bravo.' Since she could talk to herself, since she could shout 'Bravo' with the others, all was not lost. What would you like, old woman? Four pancakes. Beef on the tongue, the taste of curdled milk, revulsions, pangs of hunger, heaviness in the stomach, waves of nausea . . . I've taken calomel, I've messed myself, she said with a disingenuous whimper. But the idea of the little girl being purged had no power of consolation, and the thought of going to the soup kitchen would never cross her mind. She drank a glass of water sweetened with the quarter cube of sugar, then felt like throwing up. Her dead would turn in their graves if they could see her at her doll's tea party. But she, long accustomed to being her own accomplice, mistress as well as victim of the situation – she laughed. Degradation, she said emphatically. That was the title of the play she announced every night to her darkened room. But it was a cheat: the word bore no relation to anything. The money left by her dead, spent without joy, without ecstasy, without surprises, had never existed. The routine of habit goes beyond reality. Why live, unless to warm oneself in the sunlight . . . Degradation, she said again, shaping her mouth into a heart. Bunkum, since being born is already a degradation.

Chasing one another, squeaking through her entrails ran the rats. Her bowels cried out their need, and the sound was like fragments of jazz thrown into a dust-bin; one must eat to live, the tiniest insect will tell you that. Her battered hat, her shiny green coat, her tattered umbrella suggested she do something about it. Do what? she answered, pretending she was a bewildered child. All alone, like a dwarf scarcely maintaining her balance on shaky bowlegs, she ran around searching for something to sell. Not that. No, not that. No, she wasn't alone! Her loyal companion was there: the little insect in the woodwork of the sideboard or the skirting board was at his methodical task again. Oh, the relief from the apprehension that she'd have to say good-bye. The little insect, with estimable tact, had not left her after all. She listened to it as it worked away: delicacy, syncopation, the finest carving, gossamer spun in the darkness, in the darkness of the sideboard or the skirting board. Never had crystal been lighter, never had a solitary task been so conscientiously accomplished. She ate an entire cube of sugar as a toast to the methodical little insect. As soon as she got up, silence returned. She waited for what the little insect was waiting for. Was it the dream of a presence, or was it really there? The silence was worshipping the night, and that was her room's reply. The day would surely

come for the building to be torn down. Her hope
was stored in a safe place. The windowpane would
break as the attic windows crumbled, but one
shard would remain unshattered. That shard would
be herself, with her immaterial face, her well-
fleshed lips, her wise, limpid eyes as she rested
standing up, just as she was doing at this moment.
She was so old, and yet so little worn, that beauty
looked moth-eaten beside her.

She marched around her room, left-right, left-
right, changed step in military fashion, then dressed
to the right. She sang an energetic tune she had
once had to practise, making gestures like a snake
charmer above her grey hair to work up enthus-
iasm. Bang – she had stumbled. She fell across her
table and felt she had been sacrificed because she
had been living almost like other people; when
she came out of herself it made her dizzy. It had
gone, the methodical little insect, gone to prepare
for even greater, even more dedicated diligence the
following night, no doubt. She pouted and had to
keep from weeping. She had been deserted, and
it hurt. She confessed as much to herself in not
quite coagulated phrases : what's the good of looking, one must put up with what one's got, there's
always someone worse off than oneself . . . The
dripping tap water. Who had been so bold, so
impertinent as to repair the tap in the middle of the
night? She needed that sermon when she pulled
her door ajar, and now she couldn't hear the tap

out of order telling her the story of her life: that drip-drip-drip of unrelieved monotony. She opened the door. The landing wouldn't deprive her of anything, the landing would never try to trick her: the drops of water were still falling into the basin of all those being born, all those dying.

At rights with herself once more, she closed the door and fell back on her mattress. She found emotions more and more difficult to cope with: if she went on making demands on herself, all her strength would wash away. She must buy quantities and quantities at the grocer's; first she must sell something in Paris, then the glow-worms would guide her to the shop. The stone for her stomach that she'd found in the dragonfly dusk on the bank of a stream one autumn. It was a good conductor of heat, that was the explanation. But she hadn't an oven any more, no kitchen range, no gas stove. The stone would shatter if she heated it directly in the flame of the methylated spirits burner. She saw herself growing old and mad as she watched and waited for the stone to heat up in the stove. But there was a salve for her wound: she could always die now, because she had drawn all her benefits from the apricot trees in autumn. Seeing them was her whole life compressed into an instant's dream. She could see them still: pink or orange, and over the colour the lightest layer of fur. Her apricot trees, her undying adoration carried on in relays, with herself always taking over from herself to

49

continue the perpetual act of worship. It was a
man, and at the same time it was a child that she
was loving in them. The sun behind a cloud, everything so delicate. A little pepper, a little salt, three
or four roofs, a hamlet down in the valley, a rift
of brightness before the rain, and she sallied forth
to meet a multitude of futures. Bread, that was the
future. If she wanted to live then she must learn
not to eat. Take it or leave it. She would chew
on a clock; dawn was breaking, milk cans had
begun to clang, the city was on its marks for the
hurdle race ahead. The sleepless hours: they could
never drain her completely, and she could never
quite get to the bottom of them. She climbed up
on the packing case and let her head fall forward.
The guillotine blade of five in the morning brought
relief as it fell glittering on to the back of her
neck. Paris was waking up and she . . . she had
finished until the moment came for the iron Métro
gates to slither gently open again.

The first noises of morning are chilly, and she
wrapped her shawl around her. Mariette, Lisette,
Odile were sleeping far from their unveiling.
Angels, come down and pile their bowls high with
delicious sleep. Another moment and she would be
taking herself for a virgin protecting them. The
daylight was lighting up her four walls. What a
joke. What daylight does is to force its way into
anuses, to sooth ulcers, to lance abscesses. Dawn
is a treasure that dusts off the brows of dying

men : night is a cesspit for those in pain. At bar
counters, the first rum of the day was bringing
renewed vigour and squaring customers' shoulders:
night, after all, was nothing but a spider's web.
A moment of old age : her hair a confluence of
rivers, the crou-crou-crou of wood pigeons, the
leaden sheen of her memories. But the rain in the
square gardens would be younger than yesterday.
She would sell something, she would make herself
a present of a trip to the gardens in one of the
squares. Her luggage? A buttered croissant. She
laughed with her hand in front of her mouth, the
earth would be in blue in two months, and the
ageratums in their frames laughed with her. I'm
off to the flicks. Are you coming to the flicks?
Shall I take you to the flicks? She said 'flicks' to
be like them. Here then, baby, here's some nice
cream of wheat for breakfast; there's a nice ship
that brings in the day, bound from Singapore to
the Batignolles with a cargo of flicks. Sick to death
of all those silent bandstands in the parks, she
would rush to the photos outside the cinemas and
soak up some of the drama put out on display.
On Wednesdays they always changed the programme, so that on Tuesdays the photographs
outside were always neglected, abandoned : she
could pretend they were her transfer. A dark-haired
man, a blonde woman; a blonde woman, a dark-
haired man. The actor's names left her utterly indifferent : their real names for her were the names

51

of the people she saw kissing one another on the streets. Her forefinger followed the broken line of the hair, stopped up the eyesockets, crushed the mouth, or paused if the lovers' mouths were pressed together in a kiss. Prudish and indiscreet, at those moments she would look down with blind eyes at the drawing-pin in one corner of the photograph. She was a sack of stones holding itself up of its own volition, this woman who had never had anything, who had never asked for anything. If the edge of the wind had caressed her neck at that moment, had caressed her neck just below the ear, then her heart would have stopped. She would have given her life and her death for another's breath that close.

She would leave the cinema without going in, she would wander about in the square, she would take up her position near the temple of the old Porte de la Villette. In the garden in the middle of the square, she would hide inside the weeping willow and listen to what her parents used to say about her. She still lives in a dream world, what are we expected to do about it? If she doesn't snap out of it, that's her look-out. They are dead now, what am I expected to do about them? she would ask the buttons on the garden attendant's uniform. Poor lamp, you are burning low now, she said to her hands, her hands that had never lived, because they were the hands of someone entirely useless. Everything was holding back, except the early wheat sown the autumn before. February, when the fruit is spoiling on its straw and the light is as pale as the light in a loft. She crunched up two cubes of sugar in her mouth – how else was she to keep on her feet? Madness. She would grind up a soup spoon of coffee beans, and eat two slices of bread. Madness + madness = madness. By attempting to go on living, she was speeding up the coming of her end. That light suddenly, that light prophesying light to come . . . Someone was beaming the searchlight of happiness into her room. Happiness. It had been necessary for her to grow old before she could think of it unexpectedly like that, without having learned, without having ever understood what it is. Happiness is something you discover afterwards, she said categorically, as if she had been happy once.

Her liveliness restored by the two cubes of sugar, feeling lighter for that wasteful inroad upon her stores, she made the grinding of the coffee beans into a ritual celebration of the sun's return. The water was boiling, the filter was ready, when two bronzed arms spattered with plaster lifted her with a roar off the ground, made a hole in the ceiling for her – she had seen so many scaffoldings, so many workmen, during her daily walks – so that her face and her silver hair were bathed in the sunlight. The roar continued, the overhead Métro thundered around a bull ring. She came back to earth and poured the water on the coffee. Living was simple: it was no more than a few habitual actions strung on to a routine. The sun had gone, but there was a shining highlight on the chrome-plated filter. What had happened to her? It was simple: she was going to restore her strength without thinking of economy. She ate; her teeth melted with delight as they sank into the coffee-soaked bread; her stomach was a pit of pleasure – and the passing train was as frivolous as smoke. But the pencil was already beckoning before the last mouthful; figures will not wait, they are executioners intent on torturing their victim. She dozed off beside her bowl, then woke with a start. Mariette, Lisette, Odile had begun their daily traffic with the objects on their dressing-tables. She must earn her livelihood. She must earn her idleness. Now that she had eaten, a wave could come and swallow her up if it liked, her and her deficit too. Was it autumn darkening the spring? Was it spring bringing new life to autumn? The seasons always mislead us. If she could only be close to a meteorologist, become intimate with reduced visibilities due to rainfall. He would talk to her about shipping forecasts, about the state of the sky, about low-pressure areas. What was she going to look for . . . The beauties of the heavens, which were also the immensity of her own ignorance. But she didn't really believe in these great schemes for companionship. Companionship, for her, meant a man putting down his blowlamp on her bedside table. The dream was lost in the butter-coloured light being reflected off the white-wood packing case under the window. She took her lukewarm bath beside the packing case, and having decided not to hear the roar, she did not hear it.

Come closer to me, my little one, oh, come closer, hummed the packing case under the window. It was an object, but she lent it her voice so as not to be struck down by a sudden lightning flash of loneliness. This was the twentieth time since the previous evening that she had leaned over the packing case without opening it. A slow journey through her forest with its trees like tall organ pipes. Beginning of dictation. Lean over, look for him, take him out of the packing case. The baker . . . the grocer . . . the butcher . . . their joint statement: '. . . We extend credit to those who earn their livelihoods.' An affront shot at her like a bullet, a justified humiliation. She worked just as hard as all the people with jobs. She painted them on canvas, she sculptured them in marble; she mounted them, she fitted them into settings. They rose up and up, they forgot themselves as they wore themselves out at their tasks, while she followed their every movement under a magnifying glass, while she thought of nothing but them. She had trembled like a leaf the day the new assistant in the bakery, a mere child only hired that very day, was made to arrange eighty cakes in the store window. 'Give us some slack, man, give us some slack.' Lying flat

55

on their stomachs on the roof they watched to see
if the slack was coming, gazing down at the hoisted
plank from which they would do their rough cast-
ing. She had gone down into the street to see the
provider of slack. She saw a man pulling at ropes,
or letting go of them. Such knots he tied. And the
screeching of the pulleys : their death cries set one's
teeth on edge. They were joking and whistling.
She was more afraid than they were : she could see
the danger more clearly. The pulley was still
screeching, the whole thing might give way : she
stopped breathing. They could sing as they adjusted
the knot of their entire existence. Their lives were
saved without their having felt a single pang of
alarm. They all discussed the food in a certain
restaurant. That was in the days when she used
to eat a sardine or a fried egg for lunch, along with
her piece of bread. That day she had eaten no
lunch. She had stayed at the window keeping an
eye on the pulleys, on the swaying planks, and then,
going back to the table already set for lunch, she
had taken up the knife, the one she used to cut
the stewing steak up into frying steaks, and run
back to the window with a plan in mind : to cut
the rope, to escape back into her room, and wait.
But she had been spared the reality : the window
was too small. Then they had come back with another batch of the latest hits, whistling as they
scraped at the grimy façade with their trowels.

She walked to and fro near the whitewood packing case at half past seven in the morning, imitating those patient men and women in the Gare Saint-Lazare, the ones who prowled a long way from the trains, because for them the station was only a pretext. She had the right to imitate them : she had given them all her tears, all the tears she had swallowed down with a choking throat as she watched them come together with gestures and caresses. Is this all there is, she managed to ask herself. For you, this is all there is, answered the cold sweat slithering down her spine. Hooked grimly on to her handbag, stiff as a post, she fussed with them as they made up their minds. They would go into a café, they would hurry off towards the Opéra, or towards Saint-Augustin. What she had, she gave to them as they disappeared : her handbag as it fell, her hands in their black and white patched gloves. They departed in triumph. they took her whole fortune without asking for a thing. They left her the quiver in her lips, the musical laments with which she accompanied their disappearances, the ungloved hand pressed against lips whose silence was more despairing than any cry could have been.

At the ticket offices, the clerks punched a hole in the town you asked for. Go on a journey ? Go on a journey just to be blinded by the glaring intimacy of two sheets as they hung airing over a windowsill three quarters of an hour from Paris ? She would rather just close her eyes where she was. The back of her neck after the lovers had left the station: not an ulcer, not a malignant tumour, but something cold and flat. A disease of transparency, a piece of mirror from one of the women's compacts as she made her finishing touches, as she perfected her appearance while the man approached. As she went down the steps of the Gare Saint-Lazare, everyone could see in the mirror on the back of her neck what it was she lacked, what it was she had stolen. She who considered herself above lipstick and face powder . . . She didn't dare brush against anything, no matter how lightly. Not even the edging of grime and soot along the tops of the houses, that furry strip of consolation, that band of astrakhan, the answer at last to so much supplication, a black line of compassion for those who must eat out their own hearts. She would buy some gnocchi at Rey's; you were supposed to heat it up, but she chewed on it still cold: the piece of mirror on the back of her neck fell off, the city shattered, it was the city she could hear sobbing with dry eyes in cafés, in hotels, at Cook's, in the museum.

She was walking back and forth in front of the whitewood packing case because she wanted the fringes of her shawl to brush from time to time against what was awaiting her, against what she was waiting for. Hope: the opposite of death. At night she wanted him to rest, so she wrapped him up. When day came, she ran over to be near him. Then, without looking at him, without going too close, she would cover him with dew. Not so much disturbed as simply moved, she would forget what it was, who he was. Now, at seven-thirty in the morning, she murmured that he was a flock, that she was a part of that flock: a very tired lamb doing its best, still trying to stay on its diligent little legs and not lag behind. She murmured all this with so much conviction that her breath went whirling like a savage gust of wind through all the market gardeners' houses on the outskirts of the city. Then, as she murmured the same thing again, all the blue-tinged primroses for sale began to lean in the same direction. The act of love going on in her room was a gratification for the distant flowers. If an overhead Métro train whirled past to drown her shouts in its torrent of clanging metal, then she would howl out: I adore you, my adored one. But if there was only the meaningless dripping of the tap, then she would whisper: I'm here beside you, but I don't want to disturb you. One should never look at what one loves too early in the morning – the things we love are too fragile so early in the day, as fragile as the thread a spider is spinning at the edge of a wood. The delicate waves of her emotion reached so far that whole banks of snowdrops and violet leaves, in Chaville, in Meudon, would lift up their heads and quiver with interest.

She fell down in front of the packing case as though she were a private in the infantry crumpling with fatigue, shedding his rifle, his webbing, his water bottle. Her trembling body, hugging itself to the case, was saying 'no' while her head was saying 'yes': the passion of a distant misunderstanding in some far-off region where she could retain her awareness of herself, yet go beyond herself. 'My angel,' she said gravely to the creature she didn't want to disturb, employing the same tone of voice that others use when they say 'My corporation, my dignity, my security.' My angel: an expression she had picked up in the street, near the entrance of a cheap, one-night hotel. Two customers had been coming out of the hotel, two kids with brief-cases under their arms. My angel. She had pressed his hand, she had thanked him for having made love to her with those words. But her angel, her angel in the packing case was too much like the archangels, though she did not grieve for that. Waves, vibrations, a breeze, a refreshing coolness, spasms of offering in her belly that were almost pains, melting feelings in her flesh, a flame that writhed inside her. That had all stopped at twenty-five.

Her angel. Here is how she met him, how she brought him back to her room. One night she woke up with her throat dry. Day had begun to break, though it was only half past three; the birds had begun to stir. Like a pregnant woman in the grip of an irresistible fancy, she pulled on her clothes as quickly as she could, and went out to search for a summer orange in the crates full of yesterday's rotting merchandise. It had become an obsession: the summer was burning implacably in her throat, the whole city was hatching out a drama beneath its broody weight, the dawn was a layer of insipidity over a grey desert. The sun had not yet risen, but it had already begun its daily task of devastation. She made bold, though in vain, with the insides of the dust-bins; but she was afraid of stealing anything that belonged to the dust-men: it was their profession, after all, and she was only seeking to satisfy a sudden fancy. Paris at that hour in the morning, with its crushed cabbage leaves lying in the gutters, is a place forlorn. The sky looked down with its white eye, and the white roses in the florist's window were a mockery: they could do nothing against the heat, against the stifling day in preparation. She lifted the lids, looked in at what the dust-men ought to be the first to see, then replaced them without a sound. Not even a quarter of a summer orange. The stalls, the women shopping, the bunches of yellow balsam wound past her in a dream. A summer without rain, without storms, is so heavy to carry. The trees were full of presentiments too: a warning of the humid, day-long hell ahead. She would lie down, the noise of the overhead Métro would bring a little ventilation . . . She was so thirsty for an orange. Have a little patience, little girl. But she didn't want to be patient, she wanted to steal back into her room

with furtive steps. The main road was a dungeon
with wide-open doors through which floods of light
would soon come rushing in. The little side streets
were escaping towards the sea. Where were they?
Had they been imprisoned? Had they been alive
once? The façades of the houses were exchanging
across the streets. The light was already stark on
the chimney tops: stripped of shadow, they were
like crosses wandering across a graveyard. What
could she hold on to before she died of the heat?
To that big carton standing at her feet. Idiot, it
was begging you to notice it all the time your head
was in the air. It was blue, with an inscription:
'Rolande.' Perhaps it was an orange, there in front
of the tripe shop with its iron shutter down.

Under the attic window, in her room, she felt
about inside the whitewood packing case with
feverish hands. Under the mauve tissue paper,
under the lining material with its rows of pinholes,
under the layer of multicoloured scraps. Her angel,
the angel she had found in a cardboard box, in front
of an iron shutter, as the clock chimed four in the
morning. TRIPE SHOP. She could still see the letter-
ing. The dust-men were secret people; they searched
the silence with their hooks; they were important;
they separated the light from the darkness inside
dust-bins. She had stolen a march on them by
going out to look for a quarter or two of rotting
orange. They wouldn't have held it against her if
she had explained how she loved to find a single

cool lettuce leaf lying among the limp greenstuff clinging to yesterday's newspapers. If she took a train early in the morning she never dared to look at them directly or get in their way. They were bigger than ants, but more squat than ordinary men. If one had come towards her, she would show him how she was stroking her cheek with an old lettuce leaf left in the gutter. But that morning she was afraid of them. They might take it away from her. She had been hoping for a quarter of an orange and she had found a winter fur in summer. But a woman who feels the cold, walking along with her little fox around her neck in the dawn, that was quite normal after all. Not that it warmed her at all: it stank. She began to run; the light was becoming brighter; how everything babbles when something unusual happens! She ran as far as the cul-de-sac where the parked lorries stood like a line of inscrutable sphinxes. She shook out the little ragamuffin, the funny little fellow, the tiny furry creature; she banged her hobgoblin against the hood of a Berliet; a window opened slightly; the cul-de-sac reeked of mothballs. She wrapped the fox around her neck and fled. As she did so, she almost fainted, she was so moved by the silk cord, by the shape of the links, by the chain, by the tiny bell between her fingers as it tinkled out instructions on how she must fasten it so as not to lose it. The mountain pink that she became every day for a lollipop eater on a Métro platform was now lending its scent to the little fox around her neck.

She emerged with long strides into the main street, ready to slap down the first stone, the first bench, the first attic window that dared to stare at them. Her progress was a dream, because the uniform grey of the city was the stuff of dreams. If she were to dawdle, if she were to slow up, if she were to take her little rascal for too long a walk, the dust-men would spring out at her from the buildings. She could almost hear them coming. There would be loudspeakers howling out that the fur belonged to them. She could see the back of her neck after they had taken it away from her: the livid square of that poster on the door of a grocer's. She took the fur off, then wrapped it back around her neck, trying to get used to it. That tuft, it was hanging on by no more than a thread – what if it should fall . . . It would leave a trail; the dust-men would follow the trail and insist that she gave the little fox back. Where is your big sack, they would ask. Where is your fork, your hook? She had nothing but her fingernails. There are times when a moment's hesitation can lose you everything. She tore off the tuft that was hanging by a thread, and hid it in her handbag. She felt safer again, once the extraction had been performed; but only for an instant: the tripe shop was calling after her.

As she walked past the windows of the Nouvelles-

Galeries department store she took fright again : the bread bins, the magazine racks, the pot-holders, the workboxes, the linen baskets . . . they were her family life, the strata of her past unearthed by archaeologists. It was bright day now and the pavements looked brand new. An arm, a hand, a sponge, a bucket inside a butcher's shop. The colour of the calf's tongue that she could not describe to herself was giving her a migraine : there were enemies banging with mallets inside her head whenever she tried to look for the right words. Instead, she spelled out where the little rascal around her neck had come from : t-r-i-p-e s-h-o-p. But the fox was going to disappear back to its cardboard box if she couldn't find the right words for the colour of the tongue, if she couldn't capture both things at the same time : the colour of trust, the colour of goodness in its latent state, the colour of warmth in your feet, the colour of a freshly sheared sheep, the colour of the sun between the cracks of a cattle-lorry, the colour of the flannel after a bilious attack.

Circling in her memory there rose recollections of how the bowls of coffee had tasted – more milk than coffee – at breakfast, in the mornings, after she had dusted talcum powder on to the skin where her poultice had burned it. She spread her arms, she turned so that her back was to the street and flattened herself against the shutter. They might shoot her, but the hell with it; she wanted to examine the surface of the tongue in the butcher's window while ceaselessly caressing the little rascal round her neck — for already she had learned to caress him by heart. What was there on a calf's tongue? Ah, have mercy, she thought as the mallets hammered inside her head. There was the freshness, the rainbow sheen of convalescence. Sand . . . yes, of course, fine sand on the petal of a rose with a hint of yellow at its heart. How far away they were now, those laborious and pleasurable hours spent with her tubes of paint: she had painted so many seascapes, though she hated the sea. But what she had painted best — all of them without a brush — were the thousands and thousands of sunsets she had waited for, followed and finished after they had disappeared: her altars, her sacred wafers while her parents were entertaining their Abbés. Beaches, expanses of ecstatic colour, great trains of Oklahoma — she was sobbing now. Bygone ages, civilizations, ancient tragedies — she had started running again. She clasped a tree in her arms, for the prophecy of light, for the athlete bearing the flaming torch.

She took the little fox back to her room and examined it beneath her attic window. To find something, no matter how ignorant or how learned one may be, is to dip one's finger into cerulean blue. And what she found now was warmth, relaxation, and a caressing softness. The fox had offered itself to the first comer, and she had been stronger

66

than the others. They had all been asleep and it was she who had come upon him. She kissed him, and then went on kissing him, from the tip of his muzzle to the tip of his brush. But her lips were as cold as marble: in her mind these kisses were also an act of religious meditation. She looked him up and down, then burst into her first fit of uncontrollable laughter: the amusement he filled her with was no less sincere than the love she felt for him. The trappers in Vancouver will sell you the coats off their backs without a second thought . . . Where had she read that? How did she dare make comparisons between a full-length marmot and her decrepit, shabby little tippet?

She plunged her face into her little one's naked groin and snuggled there. Who had clung to him like this in the past? Who else had kissed him until she was exhausted, oblivious of the whole world? She invented past passions for her ragamuffin as she sat with him beside the dirty dishes. She did not go out walking with him in her square, in front of her cinema, in her waiting-room, outside her café, as she had promised herself she would. Someone might recognize him, they might be separated. She made a setting for him out of her own existence, she mounted him in her private life, this brother, this child, this companion, this lover she had brought into the world. She would take him out on to the quais after dark, when the weather was warm, when the lines of lights on the pleasure boats were drifting past the flags of ivy hanging down the river wall by Notre-Dame. She would give the shopping bag in which she carried him on these jaunts a shake: the church and its towers would quiver with the music of a requiem, and the lighted pleasure boat slide silently along the Seine. They are going to come and search my room, they will find him there, she would say to herself afterwards, as she was walking past the restaurant and café terraces. Who were 'they'? Don't know, she would answer, and a feeling of sadness would well up inside her, because she knew that the fox was really nothing but a little dead animal that someone had thrown out into the gutter.

As each day passed, she kept him more and more closely confined, eventually refusing him even the flattering light of the moon. She would squander a match for him on dark and moonless nights; she would move the flame to and fro along his length, enchanted at burning her fingers for his sake. Then, in the same dark night-time, he would warm up that place behind her ear where we need other people so much. What had to happen happened: he grew more beautiful as he acquired greater value, and he gave her what she asked of him. She would run away with him, and their long trans-continental train would crush the young girl and her parents lying on the rails. The little fox, when they came back, would look into her eyes with the eager and hopeful gaze of cheap jewels.

Now that she was a mother by adoption, whose life was all caresses, transports, ecstasy, grief and pain, the slightest whiff of bindweed was enough to make her start calling this adopted child her beloved, her lover.

But now the time had come when she must sell him, offer him up for sale, part from him. It would not be difficult to sell him, for he was a unique piece. Then she could buy him back later on, later on when she had made her fortune, and she would enshrine him then in memory of the bad, dark days they had lived through together. She questioned him: could he see that it was Judas he had before him? 'Judas' is easily said; but one is obliged to look out for oneself if one wants to eat. Parting from what one loves is normal. What is there in life one doesn't have to part from? She would be with him again one day: she was going to stride over islands, over rocks, she was going to become rich. Her eyes, when the moment came to find him again, would be roses nestling among laurel leaves: he would hear her when she called to him. He would prick up his ears, they would have become two antennae sensitive even to the murmurs of rising sap in flower stems, to the snowdrop's soprano, to the alleluhia rising from a pool of violets. Tawnier than the flaming sun, he would move towards her between two hedges of trombones and tubas.

Set forward then! The sacrifice had already become a victory. What should she wrap him in before presenting him to the prospective buyer? In a sheet of brand-new paper tied with gift-wrap ribbon. Two purchases = a double folly. She rushed into that folly, she would be rushing into famine if she did not sell him. She would sell him, yes she would, there would be enough time to lament when she had the money he brought her. She had loved him, she would go on loving him. Every day, every night, she would dance round and round the packing case until she was possessed by a tom-tom; she would take his tomb in her arms and she would dance with it. She swore it, she swore she would buy him back with his own weight in gold. One must part from what one loves before one can know its true worth. She could see the whole world peopled with connoisseurs of his merits: buy Little Foxes, they're a sure thing, they're the bluest of blue chips. Figures tormented her: the lackeys of the wealth she had in her possession. There was no way out of the dilemma but this: if he succeeded, then she would succeed. They would both fly off on their own wings. Nothing ventured, nothing gained. The roar of the overhead Métro. She wondered why she still listened to that irrelevance. How was she to contact the buyer? Rome wasn't built in a day. Whenever there is a decision to make, all the old proverbs come crowding in upon you uninvited. Proverbs: a limitless capital, the income, the dividends of experience. She delved into this fund, she was reassured by this wealth; she took the

hundred and fifty francs out from between the two
tattered dishcloths.

Room to move! Space! She swept away her
breakfast dishes with the back of one hand. The
future needs plenty of room to manoeuvre in. She
set those words to music and sang them as a song
to the debris of her porcelain. The roar, I don't give
a damn for the roar, she shouted across to her
umbrella, to her hat. She was so young, so modern;
her don't-give-a-damns were emancipation. But
what was the cause she was fighting for? What was
she emancipating herself from? From her virginity?
But that suited her as much as her hair did when it
was properly combed. What piles and piles of possessions one would have to have, how stupefied by
them one would have to be to sell an iron for twenty
francs. Twenty francs. The price of a slice of bread
at the bakery. She was going to fritter it away, the
money from the sale. But it was a matter of life
and death. I am a saleswoman, she said to herself.
The wind was scouring her, she had been washed
clean, she almost had a profession. What was that
flapping and slapping at her cheek? It was like
washing hung out to dry and waving its arms in the
wind; but it was also the enterprise she was about
to undertake. She had always brushed him on high
days and holidays, she had stretched him out on
the table as it snowed, while the beggars begged
in the streets. The idea would never occur to her
that it is possible to share an icy room, to share the

71

warmth of wooden logs at a hundred francs apiece. She had no more kisses to give him : she had already given him all she had left. No more emotionalism, she must be off on her way now to the land of success – she need do no more than open a telephone book, close her eyes, lower her finger on to the page. How was it possible to feel discouraged when there were pages and pages packed with names, when to consult a telephone book was free? . . .

An hour later, the package was ready. She lunched off a slice of dried bread and some cubes of sugar, then set sail into the sunlight.

The office boy knocked once. Silence. The office boy knocked twice with restraint. Silence, silence. The office boy knocked three times, with restraint at first, then more loudly. Silence, silence, silence. The office boy knocked four times with steadily decreasing temerity. He gazed at his wedding ring in panic. She also remained silent. The office boy stood in sullen hesitation. If I don't keep on knocking, he'll fire me, he thought. If I do keep on knocking, if I wake him up, he might fire me for that too. He sees everyone, that's a principle. At such moments the office boy was always assailed by anxiety, angry with his forefinger because it was so timorous, angry with it for being too bold. He began another series of blows on the door. Being able to rest at the beginning of the afternoon was

73

a stroke of good luck, even if you weren't the boss. The office boy rejoiced at the thought that such a thing as a week-day siesta existed. Then, quite suddenly, he felt stifled by his employer's silence. He was filled with an abrupt longing for a hammer so that he could knock harder and harder still.

M. Dumont-Boigny woke up, and with his eyes still scarcely open said: 'Come in.' He was available again; his five minutes of escape had rejuvenated him.

The office boy hesitated; M. Dumont-Boigny repeated his 'come in' and sniffed his hands: they had a scent of Gournay river mud. He had had a pleasant sleep and a pleasant dream about the boat in which he had once spent his days drifting down the river as a boy.

'She's peculiar,' the office boy began.

M. Dumont-Boigny lit a cigarette. The stiffness in his elbows was irritating him. One thing at a time.

'Explain yourself,' he said, back once more with his business concerns on the rue d'Hauteville.

The office boy was trying to pinpoint the difference between the packet of Gauloises on his employer's desk and the packet of Gauloises he himself would buy in rue Popincourt on his way home. He was all dangling arms – like an old monkey. M. Dumont-Boigny, very much at his ease, was comparing sample cards. The office boy shook himself.

'She's waiting without saying anything, that's
what makes her peculiar. . . .'

'So it's a woman?' M. Dumont-Boigny cut in.

'I told you that in the beginning,' the office boy
said under his breath.

M. Dumont-Boigny was pushing away sample
cards and pulling others towards him, all with one
hand.

'I don't see what there is peculiar about being
patient. . . .'

He is taking her side without having seen her,
the office boy said accusingly to the elegant pen
stuck into the elegant penholder.

'What does she want? What does she say she's
here for?' M. Dumont-Boigny asked without lift-
ing his head from his sample card.

The office boy was dozing on the penholder. He
started.

'She was already there waiting when I came on
duty. . . .' He consulted his watch. 'That makes it
almost two hours she's been standing out there.
And she won't have anything to do with the chairs
I offer her,' he added sourly. 'She's holding a package under one arm and she says she wants to show
you what's in it.'

M. Dumont-Boigny replaced the sample card in
exactly the same spot on his desk from which he
had taken it. His cigarette was burning away in
the ashtray.

'I want to see what it is she's brought me, but

I don't want to see the woman herself,' M. Dumont-Boigny decided.

The office boy turned on his heels.

A moment later he returned with the package done up in its pretty ribbon.

'She says she wants to sell you what's inside,' he said.

He waited. He too was interested to see the contents.

M. Dumont-Boigny began meticulously untying the ribbon. He was irritated at so much mystery over a simple package.

'I'll ring for you,' he said to the office boy.

The office boy left his employer's office, inwardly blaming the strange woman for his dismissal. But he was scarcely over the threshold when there came the sound of his employer's bell recalling him.

'What am I expected to do with this?' M. Dumont-Boigny asked, thrusting the package back at him.

He seemed depressed.

The office boy rushed back out to the visitor, mad with fury and curiosity.

'Aren't you ashamed to come bothering people like this!'

He tossed the package back into her outstretched arms.

The office boy was fascinated by the Anastasia mystery. It came into his mind as soon as the strange woman left. That black overcoat turning

green . . . that round hat with the faded spots . . .
perhaps they had been made by Anastasia's tears
— if she existed, that is. He stretched himself before
going back to his desk.

My angel. Don't be sad, little angel. Innocent little angel. I wanted to part with you, to get rid of you for money, but he didn't want you, I would gladly kiss his hands, that man who didn't want you. My angel, my little angel, I have learned what I already knew: we shall spend the rest of our lives together. I shall never be parted from you. I am hugging you because one always feels cold after people have been unkind. Warm yourself up close to me, we are closer together now than candlesticks on a mantelshelf. I can't show you in broad daylight because they'd begin not wanting you again. Drink, my angel; everything I have inside me is yours, soak it up through the paper, through the sleeve of my coat. Suck my blood out of the hollow of my elbow where you are lying, where you are

78

keeping warm. It's just as you please, it will always be just as you please from now on. You're tired because I'm tired; let's sit down on one of the steps of his staircase. His double-barrelled name made me feel confident; especially the hyphen: it seemed like a link. What is he called? I've forgotten. It's true, I've forgotten.

She sat down on the second step of the cramped staircase leading up to M. Dumont-Boigny's business office in Rue d'Hauteville. Tears of love flowed from her eyes out into the courtyard, the courtyard surrounded by tiers of business offices piled one on top of the other. She had become one with her little fox, now that they had been thrown out together. The first affront had bred and multiplied until it became a thousand different affronts. But now each tear of joy was washing one of those affronts out of her. To love one another without asking each other questions. She emptied herself of everything, so as to become a simple posy of flowers. Life, oh life, she said, clasping her hands, though taking good care not to disturb the package under her arm. To be thrown out like that without being given a chance to explain, that was a misfortune. They close the door behind you, and you are in mourning for the very little that you had to tell. But the misfortune turned out to be a happiness: that was life. It was as simple as a marriage between blind people. So simple that her eyes were weeping tears of love in two long streams.

My angel, my little angel. She could forget him now, if she wished, because he was herself: her withered dugs, the threads of silver under her arms. She did forget him for a moment, as she contemplated herself lying dead of hunger and cold in a ditch; but in her vision he was still surrounded by the warmth of her arm, by the warmth of the same piece of paper tied with the same pretty ribbon, and she wept at the reassuring sight of herself lying dead – yet still not parted from him. A noise. No one must laugh at them. She hid the package containing the little fox inside her coat. But it was only the doorbell of one of the business offices upstairs; silence returned. Her little fox's eyes were round, they were boot buttons; but what was that she could see on the wall, above the staircase? A swelling, a lump of dough rising, a loaf of bread: it was him – that too was him, now that she had discovered they were never to be parted. I'm hungry but I can wait, she murmured to him gently, gently in the quiet staircase.

She took him out from inside her coat. If only she could see his eyes, two flinty sparks of gaiety since the insult they had suffered. No, she couldn't take him out from inside his paper: someone would only come by, and then they would be forced to enact the same scene all over again with a different office boy. She was bound to him forever now, why try to turn the clock back? M. Dumont-Boigny's

86

knot fell apart, the package was about to open of its own accord – it was opening. The wall, the banister, the steps, the brass ball at the bottom of the stairs, they vied with one another to see who could shriek out those words the loudest. The door mat shouted them after the others, and more distinctly : 'Aren't you ashamed to come bothering people like this!' They were all silent; the doormat had been the last to speak. And yet. When she thought about it. That page in the telephone book had been prodigal with promises. And yet. As she thought about it more. The finger she let fall upon that name had been so full of trust. She fled out into the street without opening her package.

The street after misfortunes. The eternal cinema that revives us with the spangled promise of its screen. She remembered : she had been wounded. She had already had it all out with herself : it was no longer possible for her to lose him by selling him, because she had tried it and failed. She had tried to make money from him, to abandon him, but now they were one and the same. Henceforth he would always be there, keeping warm in the crook of her arm whenever she went out. It was a long time since her dead had had a feast day. But there was no hurry for her to join her dead now that he was lying there, nice and warm, in the crook of her arm. She stood there sleeping with her eyes wide open; she stood there like an old, old child that has been punished and sent to stand at the back of the class: she turned her back to the street.

She was awakened by a baying of car horns. What was it the street had in store for her now? Portcullises were being hauled up, drawbridges were being lowered, swaying planks were being hauled into position, steps were unfolding from carriages, theatre curtains were swinging open: she turned back towards the street and held out her hand.

She kept her eyes closed a lot of the time: the endless procession of cars was tiring for them. She found herself aboard a moving train; she sat down beside herself in one of those old, jolting compartments . . . Distraught with gratitude at having found herself, she would open her eyes, see nothing in her hand, then close her eyes once more and continue with the train journey.

'Here,' a man's voice said. A cruel-sounding, severe voice. The voice of a man already regretting what he was in the act of doing.

She opened her eyes.

A well-dressed sort of man, a man of means, a man surrounded above all by that special glow that comes only from beautifully kept clothes, was putting a twenty-franc piece into her hand. The coin bounced off her palm and tinkled away across the pavement; whereupon the man picked it up and put it back in her hand again. Someone was taking care of her: she closed her eyes again.

'How sad,' he said, as though examining a case of contracted tendons rather than just looking at an outstretched hand.

He came and stood beside her, inspecting the wealth he had just donated. Then he picked up the twenty-franc piece and slipped it into the beggar-woman's pocket. After which, satisfied with his attitude towards the alms he had given, he walked off. The woman standing there straight in front of her, indifferent to the money she was begging, made him feel ill at ease.

Having succeeded once, she tried it again. This time she formed her outstretched palm into a little hollow and stared down into it, absorbed by each deep wrinkle cutting across it. It was a nest she had built for money. Nothing came. She must divert her thoughts away from the matter. She gazed at the bundles of whitish furs in a furrier's shop across the street until her mind became quite numb. The irregularly shaped skins looked like France on a map. 'Wild fells bought,' she read on the left side of the window. What were wild fells? She would leave this world without having discovered what they were. But, after all, ignorance was also a perpetual promise. Shop windows began to light up along the street: Paris was putting on its evening jewels before it was dark. She addressed herself to the bundle of whitish furs in the furrier's: 'I'm in mourning for all my things in the pawnshop,' she said aloud.

A very short woman, scarcely able to balance herself on her high heels, was halted in her tracks by the sound of a pavement whispering to her about mourning and pawnshops. Her flared skirt danced round her legs, and her big, worn carpet-bag hid one of her reddish brown stockings with golden stars on them. She took a hundred-franc note out of her notecase, checked, after giving it, to make sure the money had not dirtied her gloved fingers, then tottered off on her high heels.

The street was kind, the city was tender at that hour of the day: she was a pigeon and the passers-by were bags of corn. A hundred francs. She wept and laughed. A hundred and twenty francs. All she had to do was stretch out her hand and it came: money was so obedient. Someone whistled, and there it was, driving towards her in a sleigh all hung with bells: the bread roll, bearing down upon her with its princely air. But this time she too was able to draw herself up like a princess: she was a woman of substance who owed nothing to anyone. She had just earned a hundred and twenty francs: it was as though the future were giving her a friendly handshake. She had difficulty in closing her fingers again; they had become so rapacious.

Happily, she noted, it was still not six o'clock: she was the ribbon in a little girl's hair, fluttering in the breeze. After six, the wind in Paris grows stronger and disarranges all our principles. My beloved in my arms, my beloved I can never feed, she whispered very quietly. Her hundred and twenty francs were curing her of her hunger as she walked along between Rue d'Hauteville looking into all the bakeries and pastry shops. Six o'clock. Flirtations between daylight and lighted windows, electricity playing truant. By six in the evening, everything had been sold. She didn't want just bread, she didn't want a bar of chocolate, she had to have something really special in exchange for this money so easily earned. The last two . . . among the croissants, among the apple turnovers: her luck had been doubled. To harvest a hundred francs. She was growing; she was too big to be measured; she was brushing against the tops of the apartment houses; she could feel the soot, the grime against her cheek . . . they were her friends as she rose, weeping, high above the cemeteries. A hundred francs: domination. The bakeries were at her feet.

She went in, imitating the carefree young man she had seen walking into the furrier's an hour before.

'Don't maul them about like that; you're not supposed to touch,' the saleswoman said.

'But I'm buying them!' she answered, with a full swell of sail.

'All right, you're buying them, so!' the saleswoman said.

Her hands trembled; the two rolls fell on to the tiled floor.

'You see!' the saleswoman cried.

They looked at one another.

'Take my sins, all my sins, even the ones I don't
know about. I confess them all, because I know
you will always be there, because I know you will
always catch me in the act. I will give you what
you want : a caress for you, a blow for me. I am
your dog, and you are in your seventh heaven.'

The saleswoman came out from behind her
counter. She couldn't bear the way this customer
was looking at her.

She tried to pick up the rolls she wanted to buy,
but they just flaked and crumbled on the chess-
board of tiles.

'This mania for mauling everything . . .' the
saleswoman grumbled to herself.

'I wanted to buy them,' she said like a penitent
child.

Nimbly, the saleswoman retrieved them with a
piece of tissue paper.

At this, she turned away her head, convinced
that she had forgotten herself on the bakery floor,
convinced too that the saleswoman had a generous
heart, that she always cleaned up other people's
messes.

'Please forgive me . . . they looked so nice. I
wanted them!'

Outraged, the saleswoman cast her eye over the
green overcoat, the battered hat. She did not stare :
time is money.

With a single twisting motion of her wrists, the

saleswoman sealed the rolls inside another piece
of paper, leaving a pointed spiral sticking out at
each end.

But she derived no benefit from that delicious
moment. She was still gazing at the same spot on
the tiled floor: the money she had been given in
the street was dribbling away in diarrhoea.

'Here!' the saleswoman said, at the end of her
patience.

She took them, her two little puff pastry saints,
and embarked on an extended thank you to the
door. The bakery became an accumulating cloud
of gratitude. The saleswoman was mistrustful: was
she going to pay, this old maniac?

'Is the twenty francs enough?' the suppliant
asked.

She lined up her hundred and twenty francs on
the marble counter.

The saleswoman pushed back the twenty-franc
piece. 'It's a hundred francs,' she said by way of
farewell.

She ran out into Rue d'Hauteville, she set off
back towards the building where trying to sell, trying to part from what she loved had meant being
kicked out into the street. The rolls fell once more
from her hands.

'We're too happy, they don't want anything to
do with us,' she said to the little fox.

For a moment she allowed herself the pleasure
of pretending to abandon the food not earned with

87

the sweat of her brow. 'You'll see how much they'll miss us when we've gone!' she said to him.

But then she bent and picked them up off the pavement: the two little saints who were always falling down.

If only she could feed him, share with him, chew with him. If she could only say: one, two, three, both together now, begin! There, in the street, in a field. You see them if you shake a hedge, my angel, my little angel. You see the little insects chewing their holes in the leaves, and though they don't take any notice of one another, all the same they're together. She was lost in reverie; her fingers had confused her package with a guitar – she was almost singing to him.

'All I can do is make sure he knows what's going on,' she sighed to the bundle of white furs. She looked for a courtyard, for a porte-cochère as anonymous as the seven of diamonds she remembered having seen on a packet of diabetic toast. She halted a second time, felt a second wave of heat, and the beating of her heart suddenly filled her with panic. If, suddenly . . . if she could not eat them before she died . . . But then the dizziness and the panic passed off.

She devoured the roll that had tantalized her yesterday, the day before yesterday, last week and the week before that, dangling at the top of the tree with the last dead leaf, and as she ate it she was also swallowing the plaster from the ceiling of her room, and the wheels and the seats of the overhead Métro. She listened, she looked to see if the well dressed gentleman and the woman with the high heels were coming back to hook the gifts they had given her back out of her oesophagus with pointed fingers. But there was nothing to be seen or heard, except that the street was becoming young again as the day waned. She pushed even larger pieces into her mouth. She felt the need to pretend as she ate, to pretend that she was climbing up on the rail of the porte-cochere, that she was jumping down from it again into the courtyard, that the beast in her was taking over as she crammed the pastry into her mouth. 'All the same, we mustn't lose our heads,' she said to the earth under the paving stones of the courtyard, for the earth might snatch back the flour, the wheat, out of her mouth. She hid the other roll and chocolate in her hands and brought it up twenty times to her lips without biting into it. She went on playing her game, climbing up the gate and jumping down again, and none of the people passing took any notice, until the moment came for her to devour, to engulf the second roll as well.

There was only the width of the street between her and the Paradise Apartments . . . The noise was refreshing. Why should she deprive herself of an oasis surrounded by noise? There were people going into the Paradise Apartments, people coming out. She would be like them : she would go in there with him, for him. She had shut him away, she had deprived him of the light, she had brought him to Rue d'Hauteville and made him look ridiculous beside all the costly furs there, her little one. No, it wasn't she who had done it : it was a finger pointing to the name on a street, to a man's name. Her angel, her little angel, why shouldn't he have lived in the Paradise Apartments? She invented a past for him, she delved into her imagination; she was so stripped of everything now that she wanted to be able to give. The man in the car there, just coming out of the Paradise Apartments in a flawless curve, then driving off towards Rue du Quatre-Septembre, that was him, that was him too : the little fox fur, the lollipop eater, the man who hadn't wanted to see her in his office . . .

She withdrew into the same courtyard as before, where everything was grimy and grousy, where everything became childlike again as the gentle rain she was accustomed to in the gardens by the old Porte de la Villette began to fall inside it. She was trembling as she walked, and she promised herself never to look over towards the Paradise Apartments again.

Some creatures, when threatened, take refuge in burrows, in caves, in the bilges below the holds, in the eyes of needle, under coal heaps, under mud, behind a trigger, in the cannon's mouth. Some set to work fortifying themselves with the bone they have been gnawing, or reinforcing their bars, or

hardening their rock. She took refuge in mendicity:
the warm feel of the coin that someone would place
in her palm – a hand in hers. For a banquet she
needed five hundred francs: she settled down to
her task methodically, as methodically as the little
insect in the woodwork of the sideboard or the
skirting board. All she had to do was be patient
and keep her eyes fixed in front of her. There was
no need any more to give food to the birds – now
it was the birds who were going to feed her, crumb
after crumb. The passers-by had wings, they could
hear what her lips did not murmur: pay for my
meal, Little Father; give me enough for my meat
pie from the bakery, Little Mother. I am on the
side of light hearts and light wallets; look over here,
you too can be made light. I never gave anything
away, I deserve to be where I am. The idea did
not cross her mind that a policeman might arrest
her. 'The package under my arm is what the furriers
have thrown away as garbage,' she said to a gentleman who had dropped fifty francs into her fleshy
bowl. The stranger continued on his way without
wasting time even on a shrug; beggars usually talk
oddly, why should he express surprise? That first
fifty francs attracted a hundred more, and those
hundred and fifty became a magnet in their turn
for an additional hundred. She stowed it all carefully away, this money she was earning with ever
increasing facility; she was nursing a hoard of two
hundred and fifty francs. Life, when you take the

trouble to think about it, is an Ice Palace, she said to herself. Begging and skating. Skating and begging.

'We shall eat this evening, my little one,' she said. 'I shall smile at you, and you, you will laugh.' They said that foxes were cunning, but hers had never been so. He was her little one.

She crossed the road, then spat without spittle, as a cat spits, at another furriers window : inside, wound around a tree trunk, was another fox fur glistening in a spotlight, as imposing as a dying lion in the tawny rays of a setting sun.

'Don't look, my darling. Whatever you do, don't look,' she said to her shabby companion through the paper.

She pushed her battered hat down over her eyes, she shrugged her mouldy green coat back on to her shoulders with a twitch that made her look as though she'd been bitten by a flea, she put out her claws, and she spat out sparks of hate at that splendour basking in the window.

The man in the dairy in Rue d'Hauteville conveyed to her wordlessly that she was acceptable as a customer. She did not hesitate.

'A slice of ham, a tin of fruit cocktail, and some cream cheese,' she said.

He did not take his eyes off her : a successful female hobo, that's not something you see every day of the week. He gave her a carrier bag for her purchases, and she handed over her two hundred

and seventy francs. She sensed that he was check-
ing to make sure there was no vermin crawling
over the money.

'And here is what I owe you,' the man said.

He lined up three one-franc coins on the counter.
She accepted them as the last alms of the day.

'Good evening,' she said.

'Good evening, madame,' he replied.

And he locked the door after her, anxious to
protect himself from latecomers. And she shut away
the three francs in her handbag, anxious to protect
herself from thieves.

She lengthened her stride along Rue d'Quatre-
Septembre, imagining herself a nanny from half
a century before, with a fresh apron on . . . so
white . . over a bluish skirt, so full, so full . . . She
walked on, she opened her eyes, she discovered once
again that a glow in the sky at the end of a street
is the most fragile of prayers when we are not in
prison. She walked on, and on; her face was a
camellia as she passed a fruit seller pushing his
barrow home from the open-air market, as his
bright red apples disappearing into a side street
brought everyone's day to a close. Love me now,
since you loved me before, she said to the little fox,
taking him out of the package. Abruptly, the winter
had become implacable : a stream of colder air
suddenly emerging from the side street. The passers-
by were bending into the wind as they fled; she felt
less courageous about holding out her hand. No,

she wouldn't stop in Place de l'Opéra. She had
come there for the cakes in the Maison du Café,
for a pair of gloves Avenue de l'Opéra. Perrin for
gloves : such a reliable firm, you know. Gloves from
Perrin. She began to recite the phrase aloud; she
decided to go on reciting it without drawing breath
until she reached Place du Palais-Royal, her packages banging and bouncing against her thighs with
ever increasing violence as she progressed. She continued to recite as she walked through the rain
that had begun along Avenue de l'Opéra; she wept,
she laughed; she was a dromedary in a desert with
her bouncing packages – the rhythmic jouncing of
her rider's heels against her flanks.

She sat down on the steps of the Palais-Royal
Métro station. It was raining, she would eat dinner
out tonight, to the accompaniment of the *amens*
and *alleluhias* rising from the earth at the end of
a shower. It was raining; she tried to make herself
completely colourless, completely odourless, with
that tiny, adored object she was clutching round her
waist inside her coat. As the water streamed in
lavish cascades from her hat, she sat fainting with
pleasure at the touch of her old accquaintances :
the little bell, the chain, the links, the silk cord.
Intermission; the curtain fell. A young girl waiting
nearby was looking at her with eyes full of sadness.
To become free again she was forced to wait for
what the young girl was waiting for : a young man
with two pink tickets. She had promised : she

94

opened the front of her coat slightly and he was
sitting at the table with her for their meal of ham
and cream cheese. She smiled, and the little fox
laughed with his eyes. Around her, in a corner of
Place du Palais-Royal, the streams of country rain
fell and splashed in wild disorder. 'I'm not going to
stay here forever, you know,' she remarked to the
bright globes on their metal arms – dream fruit on
dream trees. But she did stay for another five
minutes, for the sake of her shoes, which had not
always let in the water. Then she threw down her
greasy paper and left her dining-room in a great
burst of laughter, thinking how her dining-table
would be snapped up later by a great automatic
dust-cart . . .

She walked through into the ordered beauty of
the Louvre courtyard to look at the snowy cornices
there. It seemed to be snowing decorations on to
the roofs. Was it because she had nothing beautiful
to look at at home that she tightened her fingers
round an architect's pencil as she walked across the
courtyard of the Louvre? Probably. Eating after
one has been hungry is like convalescing after being
ill.

She walked along the quais of the Left Bank
with her feet sloshing about inside her shoes, and
when she stumbled against one of the chestnut trees
it was M. Dumont-Boigny emerging from the telephone book to wound her yet again : a thick-
skinned man inside an old tree. Then, quite sud-

denly she flung her free arm around the tree, forgetting the telephone book, oblivious of M. Dumont-Boigny. Suddenly she was discovering again, as she always did, the movement, the fragility, the gentle palpitation of the lights reflected in the waters of the Seine. It was a river reflecting light, but it was also a breast heaving with emotion. She tried to explain this to the tree. The tree was deaf, but she would not give up; with her closed fist she tapped out her message on the hollows and ridges of its trunk : this continual movement of the lights on the surface of the water is the volume, the weight of a breast in a nativity. Paris, with its thousands and thousands of splintering lights, was dancing on the water. She opened her coat and compared. The little bell, the chain, the links, the dark brown silk cord. She wrapped the little fox up in his paper again, deciding that she preferred the stillness of death to glittering movement. The charcoal smudges of the trees beside the Seine brought her reassurance. What cause could she possibly have for apprehension? Her world consisted of nothing but what she had invented. Her arm was brushing against the padlocks on the booksellers' boxes; it had stopped raining; the clock swelled its throat and called out the hour in dovelike tones. She hugged the package tighter in her arms and told the little fox that the rain had stopped, just as a mother might have told a child. It had stopped in Paris, outside Paris, around them, and far into the distance. She stroked her forehead as she walked, enjoying the gentle touch of infinity against it that comes after rain. 'Good night, my little ones,' she said as she passed the towers of Notre-Dame, the organs, the Masses, the fugues, the toccatas. A dark black swarm emerged from the hanging ivy, then went back in: all the sounds that had reverberated through Notre-Dame a little while ago, or the day before. She raised her head; she had never in her life been tender, tall, and nuptial like those two towers in the sky. 'Let's get out of here,' she said to the little fox. But she didn't; she threw down her handbag and her packages on the wet wooden top of a bookseller's box and let herself sink into the dark green of its paint; she herself, with her gently beating heart, was the throbbing of that deep green colour, as deep and as calm as meditation. The whole of Rue d'Hauteville collapsing into nothing at the bottom of a dying stove.

She was accustomed to coming on foot from all over Paris to visit the River Customs building. But now the River Customs building had changed: she found herself sighing beside a compound in which lines of cars were waiting for their masters. On to the side of the building, once always secret and solitary, by day as well as by night, there had been built a shelter for two policemen. They were talking to one another, and two policemen in conversation was a sight that always sent her gliding noiselessly off into the shadows. She turned towards the cars and their drivers flashing past at sixty miles an hour. At the end of that speed lay silence; but the drivers of those missiles would never attain the dank silence of the River Customs building as it stood in contemplation of its own inner calm. She had come there three times a year for twenty years. Now there were all sorts of cars driving up and down on both sides of the entrance steps. She would not come there again.

She continued her way across Paris on foot, and eventually arrived back in her own room, with three one-franc pieces, at eleven in the evening.

Often, we melt into our ecstasies as though they were jams, as though we were sinking into syrupy bowls of gooseberries, of raspberries, of bilberries. She let herself melt into her furniture and her things. Why expend her love elsewhere when they loved her all the time, when they were waiting for her? The world is a heavy burden, and yet we carry it. As soon as we are back in our burrows, whether joyful or discontented, we close the door upon it, we turn our backs upon it. The fidelity of things is only an expression of our own infidelity. Sitting on the whitewood packing case under the little attic window, still fully dressed, her packages on her lap, she discovered that the afternoon just past had been the longest journey of her life, that her room was becoming obsolete. No time for rest after those hours and hours of walking. She was being harassed even by the pale yellow silence of a crust on the corner of the table. She threw her hat down on the mattress and rose from the packing case. Past, present, future: they were but a single toboggan, and she must cling to the bar with both hands. Desertion is not as easy as all that.

What have I done? she asked each piece of furniture, each of her possessions, as she walked slowly round the room with her packages. Her voice echoed down a long corridor formed by the pieces of furniture and the things that were threatening her. She picked up the funnel from the sideboard and blew into it: not a sound came out. What's the matter? She asked the iron bar of the little window as it rattled to draw attenion to itself. At that moment came the roar, the invader who never tired, who was always there, always ready to remind her of everything. The ribbon, the brand-new sheet of paper, herself wrapping up the little fox before she set out. She had wanted to sell him, but things had been too much for her. Those minutes this morning, these minutes now in the evening: the sameness, the virginity of time. The roar of the overhead Métro was an old acquaintance who could always be counted on for a visit. All this sad wreckage had to be transformed into a marriage feast. She put her angel to bed, she tucked his rags and old clothes around him

99

inside the packing case, and then she consented to undress. The stars were less curious than they had been the night before, except for a single eye still open among all the darkened windows of the building opposite. She was back home at last, yet she was trembling and her teeth were chattering. She told herself that it was because she was still hungry, and she began padding round and round the tin of fruit in syrup – in vain, because she had no can opener, no hammer, not even a pair of pliers. She followed the shuffling of her slippers around and around, by herself she formed a ring of hungry beggars circling the table. She counted, she decided she must stop after she had walked around the table fifteen times. She was trembling more and more, she could no longer see clearly, she felt that her furniture, her things were all leaving her. But no, that was not how she imagined death coming to her. Death was a presence in disguise who had been nibbling away at her ever since they cut her umbilical cord.

She wondered what was making her body so panicky. Ham, rolls and chocolate, cream cheese, they were all nourishing foods, and she had learned to live on almost nothing. But taking herself to task like that did no good: she was still a plum tree shaken by a gale. And the more she trembled, the more she understood what it was that had happened. She had tried to get rid of something that was indispensable to her – her little fox. She had chosen a man – Dumont-Boigny – from a page of the telephone book, so that she could sell him the thing she had adored, still adored. And that man, without having met her, without hesitation, had rejected her and set her back in the right path. An extraordinary man, that Dumont-Boigny: he had sent her away, he had saved her after she had waited hours to see him. He must be able to see into the future, his office must have walls of glass. Without a gesture, without moving from his chair, without showing his face, it was in his power to pull you aside from the thing that would rend you apart. Before long she would have been imagining him armed with a sword, a knight-errant rescuing her from her unhappiness and her grief. Liar, storyteller, braggart! Your little fox is there beside you, isn't that enough for you, you third-rate daydreamer? Who was it speaking to her like that? It was the shawl spread-eagled across the mattress on the floor. Abandoned, yes, it would have been difficult to look more abandoned than that. So much the worse. She switched off the light and held out her handbag to M. Dumont-Boigny: she had sometimes seen Negroes, and white men too, carrying their ladies' handbags in the street, or in gardens. She switched the light back on. The furniture, the room, her possessions, they none of them wanted anything to do with that sort of thing: you can't run with the hare and hunt with the hounds. M. Dumont-Boigny had been swept out of existence before even making his entrance. She became annoyed: she didn't want to recognize the fact that her walls were ready to protect her, that she was herself only when she was living alone, and that every crack in her floorboards was aware of that fact. 'Oh, you!' she cried, throwing herself at the spread-eagled shawl. But the shawl merely wriggled joyfully on the mattress.

'So I begged, what of it?' The flowers were snickering, the flowers were weeping. She had begged, and she had done well to beg. A stomach is not a rule of grammar, one has to take what comes. Everything in the room agreed with that. And also . . . You betrayed us! The shout came swelling out from the skirting board where the little insect had been working away at its methodical task the night before. Mademoiselle has been staring at mink tails – 'I was begging' – in the furriers' shops along Rue d'Hauteville . . . The sideboard laughed. Mademoiselle was eyeing – 'I was begging' – the monogrammed writing paper in a stationer's . . . The columns of the sideboard were contorted with laughter. The steel of her knife rattled out its ultimatum: if she was not in agreement with them, then it would lose its temper. She belonged to those that she belonged to, that was quite clear. Otherwise . . . She would have her throat cut. Her throat cut. Had she understood quite clearly? The furniture, the possessions, the things in her room had gone mad. In whom was she to place her trust?

Throat cut, throat cut, hummed faded traces of foliage on the carpet, which had remained neutral until that point. 'What did I do?' she asked the tattered garment hanging from a nail. You abandoned us, growled the shawl spread-eagled across the mattress on the floor. 'I went out. But I have always gone out in the daytime.' Who could gainsay that? The flower on her breakfast bowl was a nun with two petals for a face saying amen. Before, you stayed with us when you went out, the knife blade hissed. You didn't change while you were away! the doorknob spat at her. 'Have I changed?' she asked the divisions and subtractions in the margin of the newspaper with utter candour.

She put on the dressing-gown her concierge had given her, she grew taller with its train behind her, she made a tour of the room, stopping in front of each object to deliver the same speech: 'When I went out I took you with me. The sideboard that waited and leaned over the lock gates to watch the barge: that was you as well as me. The chair that rested by the Sevran-Paris bus: that was you as well as me.' Not this afternoon, the iron bar of the window howled lugubriously back at her.

'It was only a finger on the page of a telephone book,' she recalled aloud through the engulfing roar of an overhead Métro. Her afternoon was shattered into fragments inside her. Oh, the fidelity inside her for that shawl spread-eagled across the mattress on the floor, oh, the heart-rending fidelity she felt.

103

She was walking slower and slower. The furniture, her possessions, her things were so many imperial presences, and she was their subject. She knelt down beside the whitewood packing case and lifted the rags inside. Her angel, her little angel. He was asleep, his muzzle stretched a long way out in front of him, at peace after his long days of running through the countryside. He would sleep forever, and she would wear him always curled round her neck. She began wearing him right away. She went from chair to the table, from the table to the sideboard, from the sideboard to the little window, from the little window to the mattress on the floor. She stroked each of them with her finger; exchanged signs of recognition with each piece of furniture, with each thing, while the little fox continued his deep sleep round her neck. Then she folded her overcoat in four, placed it inside the whitewood packing case, set her battered hat and her handbag containing the three francs on top of it, and closed the lid. She lay down on her mattress on the floor dressed in the long dressing-gown with its train, and looked at the quivering iron stay of the little window pierced with its four holes. She did not hear the roar of the overhead Métro, nor the hours chiming out from the direction of the pancake shop.

Also published by Peter Owen

Nearer the Moon

Anaïs Nin

0 7206 1206 3 • cased • illustrated • 400pp • £25

'Fully conveys a life lived at white-hot intensity . . . a psychological and literary triumph.' – *Chicago Tribune*

A feminist icon who pushed the boundaries of women's writing in terms of both form and content, Anaïs Nin has long been celebrated for her diaries which revealed her private self, her doubts and weaknesses and the uncensored details of her relationships.

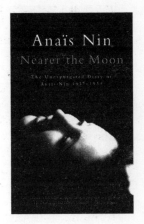

This fourth volume of *A Journal of Love* follows *Henry and June*, *Incest* and *Fire* to cover the years 1937–9 when she was aged thirty-four to thirty-six. It continues the story of what Nin called her 'dismemberment by love'.

She remains torn between three men: the writer Henry Miller, whose detached self-immersion and artistic amorality both attract and repel her; a passionate Peruvian, Gonzalo Moré, who is a sensitive and attentive but jealous lover and who drives her to distraction; and Hugh Guiler, her faithful husband.

The diary ends with Nin's departure from France as war looms. She has no idea that she will never live in France again and that this is the last diary to be written there.

Also published by Peter Owen

Two Serious Ladies

Jane Bowles

0 7206 1179 2 • paperback • 202pp • £9.95

'*Two Serious Ladies* is a work of
peculiar sharpness, originality and
power.' – *Guardian*

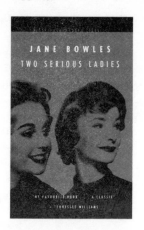

'My favourite book. I can't think of
a modern novel that seems more
likely to become a classic.'
– Tennessee Williams

'One of the finest modern writers of
fiction in any language.'
– John Ashbery, *New York Times
Book Review*

**Christina and Frieda are two staid women who want to
break out but end up breaking down in Jane Bowles's
bizarre and marvellous 1943 novel.**

Christina Goering is a wealthy spinster in pursuit of sainthood
who ends up as a high-class call-girl, while Frieda Copperfield
leaves her dull husband and heads for Panama where she falls
in love with a prostitute. Written with biting wit and cool
compassion, *Two Serious Ladies* is a bittersweet celebration of
female freedom that has been hailed as a landmark in
twentieth-century literature.

Also published by Peter Owen

Erotica
Jean Cocteau

0 7206 1181 4 • illustrated paperback • 110pp • £13.95

'These erotic drawings are replete
with Cocteau favourites –
well-endowed teenage sailors
disporting themselves in a blatantly
sexual manner . . . delectable'
– *Gay Times*

'Lavish . . . a fitting tribute to sexual
love and a defiant expression of
sexual liberty' – *Him*

**The majority of drawings in this volume – obsessional,
worshipful and sexually explicit – could not be published in
Jean Cocteau's lifetime. Before the first publication of *Erotica*
in the early 1990s, few of these images had been seen before
in Britain.**

Cocteau's models were from a variety of backgrounds. Some
were casual pick-ups, others were lovers and friends. Among
those represented here are his most famous lovers – the
precocious writer Raymond Radiguet and the actor Jean
Marais, as well as many of his distinguished contemporaries:
Picasso, Stravinsky, Nijinsky, Apollinaire, Sarah Bernhardt,
Isadora Duncan and Mistinguett, 'Queen of the Paris Music Hall'.

Highly revealing of Cocteau's search for his own personal
'truth', these sensitively drawn and haunting works have taken
their place beside the erotica of such artists as Picasso,
Modigliani, Schiele and Neizvestny.

The Miscreant

Jean Cocteau

0 7206 1173 3 • paperback • 163pp • £9.95

'Butterfly-like, brilliant, febrile . . .
Cocteau's famous novel was all but a
bible to avant-garde intellectuals of
the 1920s' – Elizabeth Bowen, *Tatler*

'It is the book's universality that
engages us: its persuasive account of
Jacques' first love affair with the
revue artiste Germaine and his
discovery that sexual behaviour is far
too complex not to contradict the
dreams of an adolescent'
– *Times Literary Supplement*

**Jacques Forrestier, the central character of Cocteau's famous
first novel of 1921, is a bisexual parasite and dilettante.**

Leaving his provincial family he comes to Paris to study for his
degree. Indulging in a life of dissipation with a group of
students and their mistresses, he falls in love with Germaine, a
chorus girl kept by a rich banker. The affair, doomed from the
start, forces Jacques to come to terms not so much with society
as he finds it but with himself.

A sparkling evocation of the Parisian scene of the 1920s, *The
Miscreant* is also a study of loneliness and youthful
disenchantment. It is a perfect showcase for the savage irony
and epigrammatic wit that consistently distinguish Cocteau's
brilliant and highly individualistic prose style.

**Translated from the French by Dorothy Williams
With illustrations by the author**